SEVEN STARS

COLLECTED STORIES

ERICA RUPPERT

TREPIDATIO
PUBLISHING

This is a work of fiction. All of the characters, names, incidents, organizations, and dialogue in this novel are either the products of the author's imagination or are used fictitiously.

The views expressed in this work are solely those of the authors and do not necessarily reflect the views of the publisher, and the publisher hereby disclaims any responsibility for them.

ISBN: 978-1-68510-138-1 (tpb)
ISBN: 978-1-68510-139-8 (ebook)
Library of Congress Catalog Number: 2024947261

First printing edition: December 13, 2024
Printed by Trepidatio Publishing in the United States of America.
Cover Artwork: Don Noble
Edited by Sean Leonard
Proofreading, Cover Layout, & Interior Layout by Scarlett R. Algee

Trepidatio Publishing, an imprint of JournalStone Publishing
3205 Sassafras Trail
Carbondale, Illinois 62901

Trepidatio books may be ordered through booksellers or by contacting:
or
JournalStone | www.journalstone.com

For Brad

CONTENTS

SEVEN STARS
COLLECTED STORIES

I.
DREAMS

GREEN GIRL

SHARP SPRING CAME, and with it mud. Cold early rains turned the still-frosty soil to a rich black paste, something that clung to your boots and spoiled the rugs. Clea didn't care that it did. After the deprivations of winter, a little mud was good for the soul. But she was surprised to find it all over the sheets.

Danny grumbled beside her as she held the covers up to examine her black-streaked legs. Specks of soil rolled on the sheets between them. She felt grains of it, still damp, beneath her hips and shoulders. She lay still as a rabbit for a moment. This was all so familiar.

The clock in the parlor chimed. Clea awoke.

***

It was only going on eight, early for a Sunday, when Clea came in barefoot from the deep, foggy yard with her hands full of wet roots and thin, springy branches. She cradled them to her chest like birds. There was life in them, waiting.

Clea walked softly down the house's center hallway, her footsteps cushioned with mud. She glanced in at Danny as she passed the bedroom, a faint curve on her dry lips, a low song in her throat. Although the shades were up for the pearly morning light, Danny still slept, wrapped in crisp white sheets, his mouth opened in a snore.

In the quiet kitchen, Clea lay her gatherings in the wide enameled sink and turned the tap on low. Cool water splashed off the tangled brown roots. She pressed the knotted things under the rising water, smiling softly at how the plane of the water distorted their lines, at the chill in her hands, at the pale blue flush that altered her skin. Dirt seamed her nails. Black grains sifted down through the clear water to sand the white enamel.

Beneath the skin of the blue, clean water, Clea bent the thin green branches into a circlet, tying the fragile ends to each other in a thick knot, tucking clumps of roots between the stems as decoration. She lifted her new crown high, dripping, and settled it on her unbrushed hair. Delicate streams ran down the curves of her cheeks and nose, dripped from her pointed chin. She wiped the drops away where they tickled and sucked the water and dirt from her fingers. Ennobled, she shucked off her robe and bottoms and walked flat-footed down the hallway to the bedroom. Crumbs of rich mud scattered in her wake.

She leaned over the bed, scenting him. Her cool hands moved in patterns over his sleeping face. He sighed like a child.

"Danny," she breathed. "Oh, Danny-boy."

He roused and rolled over, away from her, but Clea was not to be refused, not with a crown of new branches on her head and the earth itself in her teeth. She worked his nightshirt from his shoulders and used it to cover his eyes. He laughed and struggled, but not hard enough to win. When she drew him to his feet and pushed him along before her, he laughed again and toddled where she steered.

She led him out into the cold wet air to the broad stump in the middle of the long garden, which had been a tall oak until an autumn storm shattered it. She sat him down on it and, stepping quickly behind him, tugged the nightshirt down from his eyes. He looked up into the white morning sky, waiting. The damp nest of twigs scratched down his forehead as she gave the crown to him, and then he felt her fingers slip over his cheeks.

He expected something else when she used her curved dirty fingers to push roots from the crown into his eager mouth. The roots and her skin tasted of earth and damp wood, and he choked trying to swallow.

"Hush, now," Clea crooned, her chin pressing his. She licked his open lips and smiled at him. "Can you feel it yet?"

Danny's eyes bulged from the pressure in his throat, but he nodded.

She tucked her legs up between his, spread his thighs with her own. What came out of her then flowed out in a surge, black mud and roots and thin twining vines that reached for him, sucked at his flesh and found its way in. Soon the roots had spun a dense net between them, binding them one to the other at the hips.

"There you go," she whispered, riding him, biting at his ear. She pulled him close and rolled with him on the wide stump, dragging Danny over and atop her. Green rimmed the wet of his eyes like duckweed on a pond. Pale leaves opened along his jaw. He laughed around the tendrils spreading out from his face. It sounded like a song.

They grew into each other, soft earth spilling from their split skins where the wry tendrils climbed toward a distant sun. Roots wormed their way down from them into the stump, breaking up the spongy wood and driving toward the black earth below. Soon a burst of thin new trunks grew where the old oak had been, a braided column of saplings and water sprouts that suggested a bending form.

***

The clock in the parlor chimed again. Clea woke again.

She rose with clear-eyed vigor, swung her muddy legs from the bed, and padded out to the kitchen for coffee without stopping to wash. In nothing but her rumpled nightclothes, she stepped out onto the half-submerged paving stones by the back door, leaving the door unlatched to let the freshening breeze blow through the house. A fine mist dimmed the bright morning air, the day still too early for it to be burned off by the sun. She clasped her hands around her coffee mug and considered the young oak tree now rising in the center of the deep yard.

Beneath her bare feet, the earth began to warm.

"Danny!" she called loudly though the open door behind her. "Come see!"

THE QUEEN IN RED

A YEAR IS not enough time to forget,
to see my face instead of hers
when he closes his eyes.
Her girl reminds him.
But I took my vows to him, I cannot go back.

She is mine now, in status if not fact.
Revenant. Dead queen's daughter.
I would have named her differently,
Cynthia, Bianca, Alba,
but it was not my choice.

Mirror image in the flesh,
her mother's echo, to remind
him that she gave him a child
and died to do it, to remind
him that I am his second choice, to remind
him of how fine she was.
The dead are always so.
I cannot compare.

I think sometimes he pretends she is her,
their two faces confused,
the girl's scent her mother's, the rustle
of her clothes a herald
that she is alive still and waiting—
and I am made of nothing, lost
among ghosts.

She reminds him that he can engender,
that my empty belly is my fault alone.

The glass does not lie. I am still a fair woman.

I will wear my hair loose
as she does, as I did when I was a girl.
I will fold my bodice so, to show my breasts,
I will perfume my lips and tongue with sweet fruit,
lady apples to please him,
but it will not matter;
I am not her.

She reminds him
that she filled her mother once.
She is old enough to marry off
but he keeps her near.

I will name my daughter Alba, if she is born.

A year is not enough of mourning,
not for a man's desires.
Still I stay bare as a stick; he remembers
what it is to get a child on a wife, remembers
what it is to make her bloom.

> I have felt it stir and bleed away,
> twice now. Barren as old dirt.
> Nothing will grow in me, nothing
> but loathing.
> I will carry one if not the other.

It is her he wants,
whose mirrored image he still can see.

I hate her, poor orphan. She gnaws my soul.

One would think she would smell my poison
on my skin like rank sweat,
weeping from my eyes. Bitter as salt.
Better hate the man that made her, but too much depends.
I took my vows to him.
I cannot go back.

She is obedient, if nothing else,

and coddled enough not to question.
Even me. Even now.

> *Come to me here, now, my poppet, my pet—*

Her name is awkward on my tongue,
I want to say Alba, my Alba—
yet she comes.

> *Come sit with me and let me comb your hair*
> *Come sit with me and let me lace your dress*
> *Come sit with me and let me feed you from my own mouth*
> *as if you were mine.*

I have paid dear
to host this banquet.
She will eat well
of the only fruit my womb has borne.
It is not sweet.

It will be me he sees then.

Only me.

ALBA

ALBA, PRINCESS, ONLY child of a dead wife. What hope for her? Docile, dreaming, her own wants leading her away from her purpose. She knows. Desire and obedience cannot inhabit the same heart. Not without consequence. But still, she wants.

Alba is a soft girl, the early loss of her mother compensated with toys and luxuries. She is her father's souvenir, her dead mother's mirror, tall and narrow in a stark sketch of black hair and ivory pallor. But her father's new wife Irina is dusky, small, and ripe, as if to blur the memory of the other. Her body promises sons. Alba cannot compete with that in her father's affections. His memory of her mother is already washing away.

But not Alba's. She looks in the mirror each morning and misses the woman she never knew.

Irina has no time for daughters not her own, especially those who could be her sister. Alba becomes almost forgotten in her father's house, still coddled, still a pet, but now overshadowed by the new wife's lure. As a daughter she can only be offered in alliance; she cannot be his heir.

Alba watches her father's new wife obliquely, and sees the script of her own fate as a royal daughter. She sees tension begin to pull at Irina's mouth as one month after another goes by in barren blood. Then Irina is at last pregnant, and Alba watches the way the ripe woman is treated in her father's house, coddled, too, like a favorite bitch until the day she miscarries, birthing a stillborn girl. The disappointment in the house makes the air almost too thick to breathe.

Alba is not a stupid child; her mother left her depth as well as surface, and Alba thinks long on Irina's circumstance. They are, after all, close in age. Alba tries to be warm toward her father's wife, to create a common ground out of sorrow. She is lonely too.

"Sit with me, Mother," she says, laying a pillow on the wide sill of the tower window that looks over the late summer gardens. But Irina rejects her in the face of other concerns.

***

In Irina's country in the wild north, the child that kills its mother in childbirth must die too, for it has shown itself greedy for life. Irina knows Alba's past, and knows that the girl's greed is what keeps her own womb empty. She knows Alba is unnatural, and she knows what magic will end her.

But such magic costs dear. It costs the days she longs to spend as her own. Those still are fewer days than what she will forfeit if she does not bear an heir. Irina weighs her possibilities and decides. She casts her magic, listens to the old wisdom. She makes her plans.

"Forgive me for my sullenness. Walk with me in the forest," Irina asks, and the lonely girl agrees. Alba hopes this will be the thin seedling of amity between them, but her hope is ignorant and without roots. Irina has made the required sacrifices, that she should have Alba's heart to eat and let the wild beasts take the rest. Alba's days will be hers, an intimacy Alba could not imagine. Irina's possible children will be safe.

But when they reach the place she has chosen and consecrated, Irina pauses. Her predator's instincts rouse. Her fingers tap the butt of the knife sheathed up her sleeve, knowing it is already too late to draw it. There are eyes among the trees that watch their every step, every breath, eyes glinting like fractured mirrors where they catch the sun. Leaves tremble without a breeze to stir them. Shadows do not fit to the trees from which they spring. This is magic too, far different from what Irina wields. Irina cannot see the watchers but she knows she will not leave the forest unmarked in flesh or memory if she keeps on. Alba, calm as milk, seems not to notice.

"What is there, girl?"

Alba looks sweetly at Irina, a smile on her lips. There is such comfort here for her.

"I know you know. Tell me!" Irina demands.

Alba closes her eyes, then scents the air. "I do not know them," she says, "yet they are no strangers."

In the dim light the shadows gradually move and take form, arms and legs straighten to reveal manikin shapes with bright black eyes in their dust-brown faces. Not animals, not men. They wear rags and leaves and skins, hold short knives and carry spears; they are prepared to hunt. Irina grabs Alba's wrist to hold her where she stands, although Alba makes no motion to run. Irina gestures with her free hand and whispers a single word to ward the manikins away. It has no effect. Sweat stands out on her face.

"Make them go," Irina hisses in Alba's ear. "Tell them you don't need them."

Thin rumors have long echoed that Alba's mother had been so protected, that the charm was in her blood. Even Irina had heard them. She had hoped they were exaggerations.

Alba stares at the creatures, wondering, unafraid. These creatures love her. She knows this, does not know how, but their love is a thing to which she is entitled. They will not let her come to harm. She knows.

"It is alright," Alba says to the dusky creatures. "We are friends."

The manikins seem to fade into the tangle of the forest, only their sharp eyes still visible. Irina pulls on Alba's arm to steer them back the way they had come. She can read the warning. Now is the wrong time. The wrong place. There will be another time, when she is better prepared.

***

Soon Irina is pregnant again. The house fills with tense anticipation rather than joy.

While this new child grows in his wife's belly, the king negotiates a match for his Alba. It is past time for it. She is well old enough to be useful, to heal an old breach in a once profitable alliance. Alba is told the name of her future husband and told to prepare for him. She must be pleasing, she must be ripe. She must be worth her husband's father's risk in taking her.

Alba says nothing to her father's command, although she thinks long on it. She sees how thin Irina has become despite her growing belly, how drawn and pale her face is. She watches Irina's fear. She pities her. She does not want this for herself.

Irina knows that Alba watches her. She knows she will not bear a living child until Alba is gone. But Irina cannot raise a weapon against her; the inherited protection about Alba is too strong. But Irina can turn to another way, as old as the old magic and as dark in its wiles. She can disguise the knife.

Irina uses her other skills to make an apple flawless, blushing red, and poisonous. It costs her much, but it will bring her much. Once Alba tastes it, once the poison stops her heart from beating and her blood lies still in her veins, the creatures will lose all sense of her. Her protections will fail, and Irina will have her heart to eat like some rare fruit, and swallow with it all of Alba's days.

"Let us go into the forest again," Irina says to Alba. "It is so hot in the gardens, and the trees make it cool."

"Yes," Alba says, her thoughts already on other concerns.

Irina fears the forest, but there is no spot secret enough in her husband's house for such a purpose as hers. She veils her thoughts, hoping Alba's creatures will not see past them to her intentions. Irina leads them down a different path than the last time, but the ending will come all the same.

When Irina tires, they stop, and she draws from her pocket the beautiful fruit. She wipes a speck of lint away with shaking fingers and holds the apple out to the girl. "We have walked so far," she says. "You must be hungry."

The trees around them own their shadows. It is quiet here, and cool.

Alba knows what she is being given. She has thought long on it, turned the prospects in her mind like a jewel. She sees the pain and starving need in Irina's face, thinly masked with false friendship. Alba weighs the possibilities contained in Irina's plot. She can choose a quick death here in the cool green forest, or a slow one in service to her husband-to-be.

Alba takes the red fruit, turns it in her hand. Irina watches her, avid. Alba meets her stare and lifts the apple to her opened mouth. She bites it, and her eyes grow wide as the morsel falls on the back of her tongue and shuts her throat. The juice of it trickles down, sweet, the taste of the apple following her into nothingness like a memory.

Irina waits, her own breath held as Alba's stops. Her fingers crook into claws around a sliver of blade. She hopes she has hidden her purpose from the creatures, hopes she will have enough time. The forest is still as a grave. Irina bends over fallen Alba, loosens her blouse, bares her white breast for her harvest. She clears her thoughts to let the memorized chant flow free, but the spell she whispers dies on her lips as Alba's protectors coalesce from the shadows. They come armed with knives and claws and teeth of their own. Irina knows her chance is gone and runs from them, unsated, hot hate in her mouth instead of a warm heart. One possible future is wasted.

The manikins do not care that Irina has escaped. They care only for their Alba. They lift her, a multitude of small hands to bear her slender body away. Under the trees, with them, she is safe even if she does not draw breath. They know she is not lost to them. Irina did not understand her potion's subtlety. The rare poison keeps Alba still, but not ended. Her eyes remain open, reflecting patterns of leaves and shards of sky. Her pale hand still curls around the apple.

The creatures carry her deep into the forest to their home, where they have made a shrine for her in anticipation of this moment. They have carved a coffin of quartz as clear as glass, polished and shaped like the curve of arms to hold her. Fine loam covers the bottom, and moss and thickly scattered leaves, a soft bed for a sleeping princess. They knew she would need such shelter. They lay her in it like a babe into a cradle, tuck the bitten apple in with her, and close the case.

***

Time goes on; days, seasons, at last a year.

It is a year she does not live, a year her great grey eyes look into nothingness and watch it pass. She is become a traveler within her own glass coffin, always between time and more time. Her pale fingers bend around the red, red fruit, cradling it against her still heart. Her coffin's translucence is lost to dust and cobwebs, to a dappled pattern made of rain on the dust. Weeds crawl up around it. She is outside the limits of measure now, and can extend her life indefinitely, tick by precious tick. She remains unpossessed, drowsing, and almost aware.

***

In the year Alba dreams, Irina loses two more pregnancies. The second is a son born too early who drew breath for an hour before he died. She grows desperate, knowing how close her own fate hangs over her. Her king's mood changes from one of expectation to one of demand. He grows older, his own time slipping away, his opportunity for an heir with it. Even his daughter is lost. Sometimes he strikes Irina, careless in his disappointment, because she means so little to him.

To escape him for brief hours, Irina walks alone in the forest. It is safe enough now that Alba is gone. She travels the paths she knows. She wonders if her life is worth another apple for the king.

One day she pushes farther into the trees, following the merest sketch of a path. She can feel the age of the mossy trunks around her, the weight of time misting the air. She presses on through a grove of fir trees, sliding past their sagging branches into a dappled clearing. Irina stands for a moment in the sudden sunlight, letting it warm her skin. She has lost much of her color since she has become a wife.

It is a few moments before Irina notices the mottled glass coffin beneath its covering of branches. She walks to it cautiously and brushes away the powdery dust. Inside, blurred as if by water, she can make out the still form of Alba. The girl is unchanged, uncorrupted. Irina draws in a startled breath. The protections on Alba have preserved her even from poison.

Irina's mind is quick. She sees a chance she did not have before. She marks the path she took and plots for her own survival.

***

"My lord," Irina says one day after she had thought long on what to tell him. "My lord, I have heard whispers of where Alba may be."

He takes her bait. He has missed Alba, his only child. But she is also still part of his strategy. The discovered child is of far more use than those yet unborn.

The king gathers his rowdy court and makes a party of the expedition. Irina, brittle in bright dress, leads the company into the forest by an indirect path, forcing them to rely on her direction. She will hold what power she can. At times she glances over her shoulder at the loud pageant of lords and servants and the prince to whom Alba is still promised. Irina thinks him vulgar, but she is not his bride. The party laughs and jokes and sings around her, but Irina pays them little mind, leading them on, wary always of Alba's guardians. At last she stops, knowing the nobles are lost, and points to the end of their journey.

"There she is," she says, her voice low and resonant beneath the trees.

The forest is lush around Alba's coffin, but still the glint of crystal scatters through the branches. The prince alone dismounts, and with the king's permission tears away the weeds that have grown up around Alba where she rests. The prince rubs the surface of the casket clean with his yellow velvet sleeve and peers into Alba's wide-open eyes. He cries out and jumps back, shaming himself before the company.

The king laughs hard and comes up beside the young man, looking down at his lost daughter.

"Well, free her, man," he says, and beckons his party forward to help the prince lift the massive lid. Stone scrapes stone, and cool air spills over the sides of the casket. It smells sweetly of apple.

With nothing between them, the prince gazes down on Alba, appraising her. Then he bends close and touches her lightly, stroking her dark hair and running fingers over her parted lips. He slips his hands beneath her cool body and lifts her free of her tomb. As he raises her, the bit of apple falls from her between lips, burning the ground where it lands. Alba coughs in a spasm and draws breath again, and her open eyes once more see the world. The company falls back in superstitious caution. Irina watches the resurrection, fascinated and appalled. She has bought herself time.

As Alba comes awake, she looks dazedly at the faces around her until she looks up at her father's wife. Their eyes meet, their gazes hold. Alba sees clearly how tight Irina's face is drawn, the fear there, the pallor. Alba knows she has been bartered again.

Even as she allows the strange prince to lift her high, hold her up, and carry her before him on his horse, Alba's heart balks. She does not want this, she will not bear this. But she is weak from her year away, and tolerates his touch and his smell as the company sings out the miracle of her return and chatters emptily of the coming wedding. Alba does not desire the prince who will release her from one stasis into another. How could she? He is a stranger who loves not her but what she brings. She marries him at her father's will, to bind the kingdoms, to seal their fortunes. Alba leans her head back against this strange man and closes her eyes at last.

***

Time flies now. Three months from her awakening is the length of her engagement, three hours long the wedding rite, and three days full of the feasting. The guests grow fat and drunk in celebration.

But Alba is bored by it all, her prince becoming a lout in fine clothing as he guzzles rich wine, and her father a bloated pig. Nothingness is more than what this court can offer. Alba glances at Irina where she sits like a statue beside her reveling king, grey as dust and wasting away, pregnant again. Maybe this time she will bear a live son.

Alba sits at the table as she should and toys with her silver knife, crossing it with her spoon, slicing the grease still smeared on her plate. She is finished with looking at the rejoicing company. They do not matter to her. This is not what she wants. Her eyes, watching the glint of the blade, do not see whose hands place the bowl of fruit close before her. But she does see, nestled among grapes and figs and almonds, a single red apple with dew still on its skin. She glances quickly around to see who else has noticed, but they ignore her. She is not one of them. She is alone with the temptation in the sea of revelers.

She takes the apple from the bowl, the apple so smooth and perfect it can only be a thing of artifice. It fits her hand. It has been there before. Turning it, she can see where she bit into it once, a year ago. The flesh is still perfectly white, uncorrupted. Her fingers burn against its rosy skin. Alba lifts it to her lips, smiles around it at her new husband when he leers at her, and once again sinks her small sharp teeth into its flesh.

The next breath Alba draws rattles in her throat, drawing the morsel of apple down to lodge behind her tongue, to bind her again to the space between moments, to take her out of the world. As she falls, she hears Irina cry out. She cannot tell the words, only the tone of despair. Then she is gone.

***

Hands lift her, soft as wings. A shadow, she is moving, but only across distance. Time is done with her. She does not know it. Her protectors carry her gently back to the sheltering forest, to the glass coffin they kept for her should she need its refuge again. They understand the workings of her world. They lay her in it, make sure the apple is still in her hands, brush her tangled black hair smooth again. They touch her, patting her softly, affectionately, with long fingers before they close the lid once more upon her. She slips from memory into myth.

***

Years pass before her open eyes. She dreams, awake, a slow fever of motion and change, light and darkness, frost and hot sunlight. She has no memory of it. She herself is changeless. She becomes a legend: Alba, the lost girl, the lost tomb with a treasure within it, rubies and onyx, ivory and pearl. She would laugh to hear the young men whisper about her over their mugs, plotting to prove their manhood by finding her and releasing her. She is something to be acted upon, a blank canvas, clear water.

But one young man goes further than bragging. He searches beyond the rumors and bravado for the fragments of truth that straggle through old church records and royal missives. Royal himself, another prince, he has the means and the time to follow each possibility into the forest, a quest that he hopes will win him a legend of his own.

He does not truly expect to find her, not Alba. He expects barren bones. He expects some hollow reflection of the gilded tales. But with effort and a long portion of his youth, he finds the place where she lays, and at last stands in the strangeness of it. The forest clearing is hushed and lonely, lost rather than abandoned. Vines twine thickly around the glass tomb, the grave so long untended that the form inside is unseeable, her existence an act of faith. Like another prince before him, he pulls the heavy growth away, rubs at the filthy coffin to peer inside. There is a figure in there, shadowed and indistinct, still softly female.

This prince runs his fingers along the edge of the casket, feeling for the junction between body and lid. He finds it. He digs a pry-bar into the narrow slot and wedges the heavy lid up. When the seal is breached, a sweet breath escapes, a fragrance of earth and dry grasses and ripe fruit. Straining, he pushes the lid aside, rocking the coffin, rocking the still figure within. The incorrupt apple once more rolls out of Alba's hands. The bite of it once more rolls off her tongue. Her throat again opens. She gasps and closes her eyes for the first time in ages, letting her memory refill. She has felt all this before. It is no surprise to her.

But he steps back, overwhelmed, overawed. Alba rises without his help, pale within a cloak of loose black hair, and looks at him in slow, chill judgment. His fine clothes and signet betray his rank. He is a man like her father was, like her long-ago husband. Rooted to the earth, consumed with status and rule. She does not want him. She raises one white hand and waves him away.

The prince flees from her, convinced she is a vampire, a demon, a monster. He sought only to rob a grave and prove his own wit, not to resurrect a living myth. She is unnatural to still live. Her magic is not what was bargained for.

Alba is glad for the rustling silence that fills the prince's wake. She sits alone on the edge of the glass coffin as the day unspools, adjusting to the sensation of passing hours. It does not matter to her that she is alone, unanchored. She breathes deeply, evenly, reclaiming her life. She must decide what it will be now.

The falling sun gilds her, and finally she is able to slip back into the steam of time. She stands solitary, surveying the quiet forest. She knew this place once. It was safe here.

It is hard to walk, hard to begin to live again. The apple still lies in the coffin, in the cool hollow where her body had been. Alba moves a little stiffly, steps gingerly away from it, uncertain of this new course. It has been so very long.

Among the tall trunks she remembers more than sees the path she must take. She follows the bare memory of a trail to a low, ruined house. She has never been inside it, but she knows what she knows. Her mother left her this, if nothing else.

The door is gone, and much of the roof. The house has been uninhabited for many of the years she lay untouched in her coffin. Inside the crumbled house still are seven small husks, dry scraps of leather and bone, the relics of her protectors. They were faithful to her to the ends of their lives, but they could not live forever. Not like she might. The thought is too much for her. She turns away from them, unable to alter their fate.

Light streams into the house from many broken places, a lattice in the air. On the sagging mantle, a bright thing catches her eye. She lifts it into the light. It is a small statue of a slim young woman, all in white marble save the ruby heart cupped in her carved hands and the smoke quartz glint of her eyes.

Her eyes are open. They knew she would come back.

CLOSE HER LIPS WITH WAX

"THE NEXT TWO have been born," Merrith said over breakfast, stirring sugar into her tea with a long glass spoon.

Ensley raised his eyebrows as he chewed the mouthful of cake he had just taken.

He cleared his mouth with a sip of sweet wine.

"Where?"

"Outside of town. Someone on the old Mabarry farm."

"Does Mother know?"

Merrith tapped the spoon delicately against the rim of her cup.

"Not yet. She'll find out soon enough."

"How did you find out before her?" Ensley asked.

Merrith smiled, small and smug. "I have my ways," she said. "Our Mother Agnet isn't the only one with skill and secrets."

Ensley was quiet for a moment.

"You know what it means for us," he said to his sister.

Merrith would not meet his eyes. Her smile disappeared.

"What it means for all of us, in turn. When the time comes," she said, "it will all make sense."

A knock came at the front door.

"See?" Merrith said. "Here's the news now."

And she rose to let the messenger in.

***

Merrith waited for Agnet to leave to see the new children for herself.

As soon as her cart turned onto the dusty road and the creak of its springs faded in the distance, Merrith grabbed Ensley by the sleeve and dragged him to Agnet's study.

While he watched, Merrith drew the sign that unlocked the door. He began a question, but stopped himself.

"Quick now," she said, and led him inside.

She crossed the room to a plain wooden easel draped with an elaborately embroidered cloth. When she pulled the cloth away, sunlight flared on the wide, round mirror it had hidden. The surface seemed to cloud and clear, like dust swirling in water.

"Look here," Merrith said, tracing the tangled lines etched onto the glass. "I've been studying this when I can. I can understand it now. Mother doesn't know."

The mirror seemed as deep as the sea. Floating in its depths, the stars, the moon, and the distant sun spiraled around a central figure. Ensley leaned close to the mirror's surface, trying to understand what was contained in the silvered glass. Through his own reflection, he could see the face of what Agnet served, what she had promised them to. It was so beautiful, so terrifyingly beautiful, with its wide mouth full of splintered teeth and its black, infinite eyes.

He reached for the mirror, unable to look away from the image. In the glass, the beautiful thing stretched out a hand to meet his.

Merrith grabbed his shoulder, hard enough to shock him. He gasped and straightened up.

"How did it do that?" he asked.

Merrith threw the cloth back over the glass.

"Don't talk about this," she said. "And don't you dare come back in here."

Ensley leaned away from her, longing, but she steered him toward the door.

"It has the taste of you," she said. "It can't have you yet though."

***

Three days later, a young woman tapped at the front door. When Ensley opened it, she kept her eyes on the covered basket she carried against her belly.

"Yes?" Ensley asked. He already knew what she brought, and he stifled a sigh.

"Send her back to me," Agnet said from the parlor before the woman could speak. Ensley pointed the way, and the woman went without a word. He trailed after her and waited just outside the door.

Agnet smiled at the baby squirming in its basket. She tugged the blankets away from its kicking legs, nodding.

"It's a fat one," she said. "Good. But where's the other?"

The woman sidled up beside Agnet and drew the covers back around her child.

"Home," she said. She drew a deep breath that shuddered in her throat. "I'm keeping her."

Agnet gripped the woman's thin wrist, squeezing until she felt the bones move beneath her fingers.

"That is not the agreement, Lida," she said, calm as a stone.

The woman resisted Agnet's grasp, trying to draw her arm back. Agnet let her go.

"You act as if this is not their purpose. As if we would harm them," Agnet said, her hands moving in delicate gestures.

"No, Mother, I know you would not," Lida said quickly, bowing her head. "But surely there will be another. There always is, and it doesn't have to be twins, does it? I love her so much."

Lida's voice quavered on the last, rushed words.

"Ah," Agnet said. "You misunderstand."

She placed her hand upon the woman's head. A pale glow spread beneath her palm. "They both will be loved more dearly than you can imagine."

Lida trembled.

"Mother, I—" she said, and slumped forward onto her knees.

Agnet put her foot on Lida's shoulder and nudged her, gently, until she toppled over in a sprawl of long hair and tangled skirts. Her eyes were wide open, staring into nothing, her mouth a slack, silent howl.

"Ensley," Agnet called. "I've got something for you to do."

***

Merrith helped Ensley arrange Lida's stiffening body on the table in his room. She chose not to look at the bright instruments laid out on a clean white cloth beside it.

"I didn't think Mother would kill her," Ensley said softly, stroking Lida's black hair back from her cold face.

Merrith barked out a short, angry laugh.

"Why would you think she wouldn't? She knew what was expected of her, and she failed to deliver it."

Ensley shrugged. "I thought Mother liked Lida," he said.

"She likes them all, or did you forget?" Merrith asked. Her voice softened. "Remember Treva, and Silane, and Megre? She liked them all, very much, when they did what she wanted. She likes us too. But it doesn't mean anything in the end."

Ensley shrugged again.

"Someday it will," he said.

Merrith swallowed. She looked as if she might cry.

"Are you ready then?" she asked. "We have to do this right the first time."

He nodded.

Merrith pulled a closely folded paper from her pocket and smoothed it flat on the edge of the table. She knew the mysteries marked upon it. She knew what they might do, what they should do. She hesitated, gathering herself.

"Here," she said after a long moment, pointing to one of the patterns sketched across it in dizzying intersections. "It starts here."

***

When his time came, Ensley knelt before Agnet, sneaking glances at the mirror behind her when her sweeping movements revealed it. To read that cosmology, to reach that center, was his reason for being. He was to translate it for Agnet, like a key to a cipher.

The snatches of it he could see almost made sense to him. Parts of it were scribed across his own skin now, and Merrith's. His sister had taught herself the workings that Agnet thought were hers alone. Merrith had always been quick and cunning. He hoped she was also correct in her calculations.

"Ensley," Agnet said at last. "Are you willing?"

"Yes, Mother," he answered.

He squeezed his eyes shut, waiting for Agnet to begin the ceremony, waiting to feel the feathery touch of her hands upon his head, waiting to hear her murmur the sacred words that would dissolve him into the divine light and open the way for Merrith to follow, waiting to find out where their new secret maps would take them.

It would not be where Agnet thought they would go.

His skin burned where the lines marked him.

As Agnet laid her hands upon him, he flinched. He wondered if Merrith was as frightened as he was while she stood silently by the wall, waiting for her own turn, hoping they had done this right.

Then Agnet spoke, and it was all light, and nothing.

***

In the empty, darkened room, Lida stirred. She woke without waking. Her cold muscles contracted, bringing her off the table and onto her feet, moving her stiffened limbs across the floor. Within her corpse, she wondered briefly at her mobility before the faint spark of awareness flickered and burned out. Lida was gone. But the shining lines carefully scratched into her skin would not let her body rest.

What drove her was not her own fading, cloudy desire. Something else nestled beneath her ribs, another motive, another will. It moved with her, and through her, even as she herself dimmed to nothing.

She walked through the house, noiseless, unbreathing, implacable as the tides, as the rising sun. Around her, the small sounds of the house hushed, as if the world within its walls waited for her unnatural presence to end. She walked past the rooms where Ensley and Merrith had lived and labored for this to be.

She stepped into the room where Agnet kept the shrouded glass.

Agnet looked up from her charts, startled, a drop of ink shaken loose from her pen falling in a blot across her carefully drawn figures. The figures disappeared into the blue liquid, useless.

For a moment Agnet froze, not wanting to believe what she saw. She had never taught anyone how to make these lines, how to empower them, how to shape the energies of what she worshipped. But she knew, somehow, the last two children had learned. How had she missed it? How had they hidden it from her, even at the end?

I will have to start over, she thought. She rose slowly.

Lida did not move.

Agnet read the half-familiar symbols written on Lida's body, uncertain of their finer nuances, and considered what sway she could have over a dead woman. She could only try.

She drew a long breath and raised her hands through the air at an abrupt angle, shifting her feet to make her own body into the pattern she hoped was the one she needed. She held it, waiting. Her body ached with the strain as time stretched on, meaningless.

Nothing answered her.

When Lida opened her eyes to show the black void where no stars hung, Agnet let her hands fall to her sides and bowed her head. She held her breath, powerless against what would come.

***

There was no one to lay out Agnet's body. It stayed crumpled where it had fallen.

Lida's corpse made its way to the nursery and crouched down between her children, cradling them in hard, cold arms. The babies wriggled and fussed, wanting comfort, wanting warmth.

Lida was past that. The forces that moved her faded, spent. The grey light that filled her flowed from the scores in her skin in fine threads, lengthening, twisting, weaving a web around her and her children. The web tightened into a cocoon, strand after strand, binding the light that made it, shrinking as Lida's corpse was consumed to construct it.

Inside, safe, two small bodies breathed.

FOR THE NIGHT IS LONG, AND I AM LOST WITHOUT YOU

THE BLIND THING that was Dena stirred its hands in tight, proscribed circles and curves, moving the water in patterns she could only feel. She willed her eyes to stay shut against the temptation to read what she had written. What needed to see, would see. A film of oil rode the water's surface and coated her fingers as she trailed them. She was cold in the cave's still air, cold in the water. She repeated the patterns as her hands grew numb. Then she wrote the patterns a third time, slowly, so there would be no mistake.

"Femina. Coniunx. Mater Caeca," came the women's voices, slushy with echoes, and under them the sound of something heavy sliding over a smooth surface. She could feel the water around her ripple, rise, as if a large body had sunk beneath the surface. Her skin prickled in anticipation of something sliding over her, but nothing did. She strained to hear more but was left in silence. She stilled her hands, held her breath, waiting for a response. A click of metal on stone like the turn of a lock echoed, and a sense of great emptiness came over her in a wave. The task was finished.

The blind thing opened its eyes and, sighted, was Dena again. She had assumed she stood in darkness, but the space around her was bright with reflected light. The cave was not a cave, but a room made of glass. The stars above her shone like flecks of ice in a hard sky. They picked light from windowpanes and scrolling metal in flares and spangles. She stood up to her hips in the black water of an oblong, white-tiled swimming pool. Currents tickled her ankles. She imagined fish drifting past her in the darkness, giant, pale carp grazing the pool's mucky bottom.

She turned around carefully, wary of her footing. She could not see the speakers, her companions. Above her, the cold moon glowed with enough light to cast sharp shadows.

"Hello?" she called out. Her voice came back to her, weaker, softer. Nothing answered.

She waded out of the pool. One wall of the great glass room was solid and familiar, shared with the main house. A plain door in that wall stood ajar, and she could see lamplight in the long hallway beyond. She had walked down that hall, to that door, many times, had often tried the handle. It had always been locked.

Dena felt loneliness sweep in like a breeze against her cheek. The women who had brought her here could not have left so suddenly or so silently. Yet she had no sense of anyone in the house beyond her. Surely Maggie was still about, Dena thought, back in her cool bedroom undoing her braids. She trembled, wary of crossing back over the threshold, in case her sense became truth. With a glance at the looming stars, she stepped forward.

As she entered the house, the great swell of isolation washed over her and away. Far inside she heard the noise of the other women moving about as they put away the trappings of the ceremony. She broke through a veil of dusty cobwebs that had amassed in her absence, then trekked down the long hall to her room to change into dry clothes and help them set the house back in order for the coming day.

***

"Why did you come for me?" Dena asked.

"You heard the call."

Dena thought Livia was being purposefully dense. Livia was the oldest of the three women Dena usually thought of as The Sisters, although she did not suspect any relation. Livia's hair was pale blonde and twisted tightly up in a crown around her head. The severe style made her look like the crone she often acted, although she was probably barely forty.

"No," Dena said. "Why me? Why not one of you?"

"Because we were not called."

"But then how are you here?"

"Arrangements needed to be made," Livia said. "We knew in our times, so we came and learned what we needed to make a place ready for you." Livia folded her hands against her breasts. "Don't be so obstinate. You knew it too."

***

Before she had found this new purpose, Dena considered herself a confessional surrealist poet. She supported herself as a university tutor to make time for her art. She lived sparingly. Several years earlier she had managed to publish a chapbook titled *Dissolution*, from which she would perform readings less and less occasionally.

Dark haired, fever-eyed Anna had attended Dena's last reading at the public library. There she had cornered Dena to flatter her and engage her with questions about her art. At the time, Anna seemed interested and interesting. Avid, even. Anna had invited her to the grey mansion where she lived with a group of like-minded women. Hungry, Dena had come.

Dena read her poetry to the three women in the house, and in turn they had read from their books in a mash of English, mangled Latin, and a wet, spongy language Dena had never heard before. At first she had thought the women over-dramatic, fabulist, slightly mad. But there was a strange pull to what they said to her in their many voices, like something lonely crying without hope of friendship. She took her turn reading their books, even when the words were too thick for her tongue to manage and the meaning made her eyes sting. But the women encouraged her, touched her hands as she held the books, gave her a place in their ritual. Her own writing changed under their influence, became dreamier, less studiedly clever, and more wishful. Eventually, she stopped writing altogether and only read, although she was never quite sure she understood.

Dena moved in, seeking clarity. It always escaped.

Her quest to grasp how they defined their answers still seemed romantic then, allowing her to inhabit their city-wrapped mansion like distant royalty. But the bloom of such romance faded with time and familiarity, and became rote demonstrations of an assumed faith. Dena admitted to herself in secret that it was an easier path than chasing poetry.

***

"Why are the prayers in Latin? I imagined something...older. Less churchy," she said.

Livia stirred the soup. "What's older than a dead language?"

Dena laughed, but Livia only watched her through the steam with a curious twist to her mouth.

"And what about the nonsense chant, how old is that?" Dena asked, still laughing.

"Do you think we invented this?" Livia said at last when Dena had quieted. "Do you think we invited you in because we are your friends?"

***

Dena knew she dreamed, knew that she flailed in her bed alone in the clinging darkness. Her mouth felt full of dust, burying her voice. The sheets bound her in place, and she struggled to be free of their damp clutch.

Under her digging hands the bedding was not cloth. Slippery, cold, what she touched was flesh that gave like a sopping sponge where she tried to grip it, too slick for her to hold. The chill of it frightened her, but she was too late to refuse the embrace tightening around her hips and her waist.

The cold pressed into her, heavy, distending her belly as the pulpy mass flowed up. Her skin split like an overripe melon, too big, too full. What spilled out was not formed, its gleaming black skin ebbing and flowing with a quick pulse. The amorphous product flowed away from her, seeking escape, surging against the door. Dena sat up, dreaming and awake.

The thing that crouched trembling on the doorstep could not be real. Flesh could not be bent that way. Black and decorated with the glimmer of stars.

Dena screamed against the muffled weight of her own tongue, choking on the cold threads and tendrils rolling over it. The air rippled around her. She was alone in her room.

***

"It's time now," Anna said. "We've waited. He's waited."

"How long?" Dena said.

Anna looked at her sideways. "Time isn't measured like that."

Dena put her head down.

"How many before me then?"

Anna folded the towel and smoothed it as she put it in the drawer. "I don't know. The records only go back so far. The last before you was in 1871. The last time the time was right. Before then, I think in the 1700s, maybe before."

Dena nodded. We want to give a history to things, she thought, that are too young to bear any responsibility.

"Has this ever succeeded?" she asked.

Anna stopped her hands' nervous motion. "Once. But not here."

***

The Sisters told her the ritual had taken, that the time had been right. They read their books, studied the motion of the stars, and were certain. Dena accepted their answer as truth. It was easy.

She lay in the darkness with her hands on her flat belly, sure she felt something turn within her. How fast would her passenger grow, she wondered, this foreign seed, this godling.

The house around her was as silent as the mystery within her. Even if one of the Sisters had been awake to ask, they would not have any more of an answer.

***

Instead of becoming full and fleshy, Dena grew so spare that her ribs cast shadows beneath them. What she fed within her took everything and searched for more. Dena could feel what she carried moving through her sometimes, like a quick-growing vine. Other times it was utterly still, and she a walking shell.

Grey-eyed Maggie brought her porridgy broth and heavy stews, trying to keep the weight on her. "It's no good if you can't survive to the birth," she said, practical, devout. Dena ate, but the thing in her ate more.

"There's nothing there," she said to Maggie one grey afternoon, afraid of her sunken belly.

"Sometimes there isn't," Maggie said. "It'll be back."

Dena kept her hand flat against the drum of her skin. How could you ever know, she thought, more sad than not.

"Are you and Anna sisters?" she asked suddenly, as if the question had been waiting behind her thin lips.

Maggie laughed then, a real laugh, and Dena could see a bright sliver of who she once had been.

"Not us," Maggie said. "Despite the hair color and the freckles. Just one of those coincidences that happens if something goes on long enough."

***

The clouds thinned and opened in an oval; framed and veiled within them was the thin disk of the moon against the grey afternoon light. Dena gazed at it from a tall, uncurtained window, unsettled and restless.

The Sisters came and went as they pleased and made no restrictions on her, but Dena preferred to stay in the confines of the house. She even avoided the small ornamental garden on the western side. The closeness of the plants, the dry enveloping stalks bounded by high iron fencing, made her feel claustrophobic.

Instead she walked the mansion's wide halls to stave off boredom and contempt, watching autumn rot into winter in the park across the boulevard. She could not remember seeing spring come, or summer. The light through the tall windows seemed always dulled by clouds. Occasionally she saw a car pass, or a pedestrian stroll by, but the activity was all far removed from her. The window glass kept her safe and separate from whatever else went on in the world. Dena remembered the other side of the glass, the sounds, the scents, the noises and clatter of other people. She didn't miss the cacophony, didn't miss the demands on her attention, the mundane expectations. But she thought it strange that she was so often left alone, when the house had promised company. An ill-tempered loneliness dogged her. Dena disliked the other women as much as she disliked the solitude.

She laced her fingers over the hollow between her hip bones and kept walking.

***

Her knees and elbows were great knots on her skinny limbs as what she carried grew. She felt like a knobby root, waiting to push out a pale tendril when the soil warmed enough. This was not the promised glow of coming motherhood. This was purely gestation.

***

Dena thought it was another dream at first, the strange holy birth sweeping through her like some terrible storm. Then the wracking cramps hit her, and she vomited over the side of the bed. She got up as the cramps eased, careful not to step in her own mess.

"Livia? Maggie?" Her voice was too thick to carry. She needed to get The Sisters. She needed help. There were still rites to be done.

The pain bent her like hot wire, clots and black fluid sluicing from her to splash on her feet. She dropped to the floor like a dead bird, the cold tiles soothing to her feverish skin. The stabbing pain ebbed away. She had the deep sense that this was not a birth at all.

Dena crawled until she reached a wall and used it to stand. "Maggie? Anna? Anyone, please," Dena called. Her own voice echoed back to her.

She held herself up with the wall and made her way out into the hallway. Cobwebs hung like shadows from the corners. The boards beneath her feet were soft with dust. Time measured itself differently here.

Her shadow crawled ahead of her like a spider.

The pain was less now, with her belly empty. An alien instinct urged her down the hallway to the door. Tonight, the door was not locked. She twisted the knob and let herself fall into the cool, bright darkness.

The place was abandoned. The windowed walls and roof had cracked and fallen, leaving the pool exposed to the night and the icy stars. Dena lay still for a moment, drawing in deep breaths of the damp air. Shards gritted under her. Her nightgown was soaked in black blood and clung to her legs like swaddling. She peeled the cloth away from her skin and made herself stand again.

The ritual had its demands. She was past refusing them. Her stick-thin legs shook under her as she walked around the edge of the pool.

The pool was almost empty, drained to a sheet of liquid over a thin black muck. Still, the glassy stars shimmered on the oily surface, the baleful moon floated there. She walked silently through the empty space, shadows flowing before her like mercury. Broken glass scattered across the pool room's tiles, and she trod carefully to miss the shards. Still, unseen slivers drew blood, and her path was traced in red.

She looked up through the shattered roof panes at the true moon, the real stars. There was no comfort there, only the promise of endless cold.

Despite the water's level, ripples lapped against the sides of the pool with a metronome's beat, ringing dull cadence in the hushed night. The even tempo lured her with its calmness, and Dena stepped down into the slippery mess. It covered her to the knees as she walked down the inclined floor, deeper than she had judged.

Dena stood in the greasy water, letting the ripples lap against her wasted legs. She could understand the pattern in the ripples. She had written them herself, had felt them flow around her, and knew what they called. She shuddered. Tears welled up in her eyes, provoked by a slippery new fear. It was too late to flee back to the house. She still stood in the pool when the call was answered.

The metal frame of the room trembled and warped and gave before its coming, and she screamed, choking on spittle.

Sudden light blinded her, pouring from the high moon like water surging over a fall. Sharp fragments of glass still trapped in their frames crumbled in the weight of the light and fell over her like dry snow.

The white light splashed over her like acid, and she felt the brilliance eat into her skin, run down her bones. Dena thought she was still screaming, but she could not hear her own voice. She lost her footing, fell with a splash into the shallows. Her throat swelled and tore as the light slid in, slick and cold as the water. She felt her lungs fill, and the chambers of her heart. The light looked out of her failing eyes at the pool, at the glass, at the wide night above, and receded like the tide.

The husk that had been Dena lay in the empty silence, a blind thing in truth, the greasy water dissolving what little was left after the light was gone.

***

Livia opened the door from the house slowly, ready to speak the words that barred it against the endlessly hungry thing she served. But the pool room was as still as ages. Stars flickered in the sky, making patchwork of Dena's empty bones.

This had not been her time.

AND LUCY FELL

IF I AM mad, it is because I cannot taste your mouth.

These nights end too soon, each dawn coming without you touching me. You come so close. I hear your nails scratch against the walls, I hear you breathing out there. I open my mouth in hope, press it to the walls that separate us, kiss the cold wet stone. No matter my imaginings, it does not taste of you.

If I am mad, it is because I cannot reach past the bars to touch you.

Cold iron holds you back, sealing your hot sharp mouth away from me. Your bandy arms. Your grasping hands.

Every night I know you are there, just beyond the damned iron bars. Waiting.

But the smell of iron cannot bury the smell of you. Your reek is like a smoky weight in my lungs. Your breath is vapor on the black air, rich as old roses, heavy as peonies. I am drunk with you. You are heady enough to sustain me through any madness, with your rough, red sighs and your hard, white teeth.

I cannot touch you. But I have not been idle while I wait. Pining is for the weak.

Every night I scrape away at the stone where the bars are socketed, wearing away my fingerprints, turning the stone to mud with my thin blood.

And my blood *is* thin, wasted and dilute with waiting. How many times have I ripped my own veins wide with my own imperfect teeth to wash the stone sill for you, to give you my strength to lap up?

And all that has come of it is a black tar on the windowsill where it dried untasted, and my teeth pulled out to save me from myself.

They tied me to my bed, but even without teeth I could chew through their ties. When they chained me, I twisted like a worm on a hook, wearing holes in my skin, straining the metal until it snapped. They did not try to bind me again. They locked the door, and they did not come back. I think they hoped that these walls and these bars would hold me. But enough time will crumble anything they can devise. Even this cage.

Last night, near dawn, the left-hand bar turned loose in its socket. I spent the day awake, worrying it, greasing the stone with what seeps from me. Now the bar is free.

I would fly to you, but before they left me alone for good they cut my wings away. No amount of persistence will grow them back. I have tried.

So now when night comes down again, I will remove the bar and wait for you one last time. And when I finally taste you in the air outside, I will sing out, Come in, love, come in, and show me what you have done with the gifts I gave you. Wrap me in your arms and claws and tattered wings. Let me see your teeth.

COMPLINE

IT'S REALLY WINTER now. The ground is impenetrable, the air too bitter to breathe.

We spent Christmas week digging graves. First Cissi died, then the cats, one after the other. Cissi was only three. It would have been safer to burn them all, but I didn't know what winter would bring. The last few were hard. I didn't want to waste the wood. I'm sick of being cold. We piled rocks over the graves instead and hoped for an early spring.

It was hard on Ben. He had always loved the holidays.

The children were all alive the year the power went out for good. Ben drew us a tree on an old bedsheet, and we tacked it to the wall and pinned ornaments to it. In the short days, the balls caught the light and sparkled. At night, they were dull as stones. We hung the sheet again this year, but there were no gifts to go with it. Not with Cissi gone. I couldn't bear it. I thought she would be the one who lived.

I miss my children. They had their father's joy in celebrating. When Tom and Ben Junior and Dahlia were still small, Ben would let them dance Ring Around the Rosie around a real tree until they were all laughing too hard to go on. I would watch and clap in time. The dancing was Ben's.

We burned Tom and Ben Junior and Dahlia two summers ago, when they came back. No worry about the cold then.

I want to let go of all the old holidays, but Ben isn't ready. Not yet.

In bed tonight, in the quiet darkness, Ben reached up and touched my face. "Shh, Mary, can you hear it?"

I could, but I lied. I wanted him to have the wonder of it. "Hear what?"

"The church bells."

No one rings the bells anymore. It's only the wind. The church has been empty for years. Ben still goes up there sometimes, mostly in the spring. Sometimes he stays up there the whole day, alone with the broken pews. He says it gives him a sense of continuity.

I wrapped my hand over his.

"Yes," I said. "There they are."

He slid his hand down to my belly, trying to stir me. I stopped him. It's too hard to keep trying if we have to bury them all.

We lay like that for a while, watching the stars through the unshaded window. I miss my family, my children. So many gone. I couldn't protect any of them. Everything gets taken away.

Ben sang carols just under his breath. I felt myself drifting.

A thin scraping rattled along the front of the house. Ben did not seem to notice it.

"Everything's locked?" I said across his reverie.

"Yes," he said.

I got up anyway to check. The moon was bright. The window glass was icy when I pressed against it to look out. I could see the orange cat on the porch with dirt and frost in his fur, scratching to be let in.

"What is it?" Ben called down, his voice drowning out the faint bells. The cat looked up at me from sunken, cloudy eyes. Poor thing. Habit must have brought it here. I don't think it could know what it wanted.

"Nothing," I said. I hope he heard me. I hope he goes to sleep.

I'm going to wait down here awhile. The night is quiet. The cat watches me. It's past feeling the cold. But habits are strong things.

When Cissi comes home, I'm opening the door.

To Selareme

THE DLSARII CAME out of the glare of the sun, swaying across the scrub on the high backs of the grey dlkii. The great beasts were patient and oddly graceful. Their massy silhouettes were distorted by the flapping banners that draped them, making the dlkii seem like winged things rather than the ponderous earthbound creatures they were. The caravan was still too far off for any watchers to make out the riders. But Thes knew they were there, just out of reach, and his stomach clenched in anticipation of their arrival.

Years ago, after the war had cooled, the Dlsarii had resumed their wandering. They went back to their old trades and left the attempts at rebuilding to the rest. Thes's father often said they were the smart ones in this, that the war had changed things so much that the world could not continue as it had been. Still, Thes's family stayed in Miridaj and rebuilt what they could.

The mountains that the Dlsarii crossed were the uneven edge of the horizon, melted into haze. Thes had never been that far out of the city, although his father had told him of wandering as far as their foothills when he was young and wild. Thes was at his heart afraid to venture so far from the sheltering city walls. He would never speak it, though, never admit even in the silent darkness of his bed that the vastness of the plains and mountains made him seem too small to survive it. He joked and boasted to his friends, but he never would venture out.

When morning came, the Dlsarii were there, just outside the city. Their parti-colored tents had blossomed overnight from the dry fields. Thes went with a pack of other children to stare from the ends of the streets. Safe among the crowd, he shaded his eyes and watched the Dlsarii go about their unpacking.

"What do you think they've got?" he said to his friend Ems as they stood elbow to elbow.

Ems shoved him lightly, maintaining dominance.

"What do you think? Probably cloth and jewelry, decorations and stuff. Same every year, my dad says."

"They don't come every year," Thes said.

"Well, they used to," Ems said.

Eventually the pack of children dissolved back into the city. Thes kicked at the dirt as he walked back to his father's shop. He let himself in to the narrow, cluttered room, put on the heavy leather apron and gloves, and began to file away the rough burrs on the edges of a cut pipe.

In the afternoon, his father came in and dismissed him. The Dlsarri were in town. He should go up to the marketplace to see them.

The sun was hot, and the streets glistened where they had been oiled to keep the dust down. Thes dawdled, wanting to string out the excitement. Then he reached the open square, and stopped in the shade of a shop awning.

Thes stared, fascinated, at the Dlsarii families that drifted through the market. They were golden brown like good bread, with light eyes and hair the color of bones. Men and women alike wore their hair long and loose and decorated with tiny, colored glass beads that made music as they walked. Their clothes were hemmed with bells and copper mirrors. They moved smoothly and melodically over the broken remnants of pavement, never losing their footing, even the wide-eyed children as they looked around at the strange honeycomb of Miridaj.

When the visitors passed through on their way back to their camp, the normal buzz of the street filled up the empty air behind them. Thes stayed where he was beneath the awning, his face turned east, daydreaming. He always had his eyes on the horizon, waiting for something *other* to spill over it and change the world. He wondered if this was it. They seemed foreign enough to change things. He could hope.

***

Two days passed. Thes had to force the idea of Dlsarii magic out of his head to get anything done, but it still stained his thoughts. He believed he was ready when the girl stopped in front of his father's shop and looked through the clear pane of the door at him where he stood at the buzzing grindwheel. The sparks it threw were like stars in the air. She pressed a hand against the scratched glass, a request.

He put down the mower blade he was sharpening and opened the door for her. She stepped into the tiny, dim shop, pulling her loose clothes close so as not to sweep into the machinery. Her eyes were large and round, pale as ice in her brown face. When she moved, the glass beads threaded through her hair clicked and chimed. Her face was heart-shaped, her mouth small. She was nearly an adult, he thought, probably a year or two from marrying. He wondered that she was there alone.

"I saw you watching my family when we first came," she said.

He looked down at his hands, shy of her after all.

"Are you coming to the trade?"

"I think so," he said. He kept his eyes down.

"You will like it."

His eyes flickered up to her, but he quickly turned away.

"All right," he said.

He heard the door open and ease shut again. He went back to his work.

***

She smiled when she saw him at the trade, and left a younger girl with the pile of carpets she had been minding. Thes left his father haggling over a dress for his mother and walked over to meet her.

"What is your name?" she asked him.

"Thes. Albourin."

"Mine is Qarathamlimolo."

Thes stayed silent, afraid to mangle it.

"Lim," she said. "Just say 'Lim.'"

"Lim," he repeated, and she smiled again. Her eyes were as clear as water.

She glanced back over her shoulder at the girl. A Miridajian man was folding back the rugs carefully, looking at the patterns.

"I will meet you in a few days, when the trade slows. Look for me."

She did not glance back at him as she walked away.

***

When Lim at last came for him, it was half a month later. She rapped sharply on the glass door at midday. He startled and peered through the clouded glass, and threw away the remains of his lunch when he recognized her. He had thought she would not come, that she had been teasing him. His face grew hot, but he opened the door.

She waited in the street for him, under the beating sun.

"Thes," she said. "Let's walk."

Her mouth made his name into music. He wanted her to keep talking, to turn the dry city into wonder, to decorate the cramped streets with the bells of her tongue. She led him toward the wide dry fields, humming softly in cadence to their steps. Thes struggled to find a topic of conversation.

"What is over the mountains?" he said at last.

"Which mountains?" she said.

There were only the mountains before them. His temper flared, but he choked it down. Perhaps she was not mocking him.

"There," he said, pointing at the horizon.

She glanced after his gesture.

"Selareme," she said. "If you go far enough."

"How far?" he said. This was news, a fixed point. If it had a name, he could get there.

"Years," she said.

"Years is not a distance," he said, angry now, his voice rising.

She did not seem to recognize his anger. Her cool eyes remained on the distant mountains.

"The dlkii take years to bring us here from Selareme. We could not make the journey without them. How else should we measure it?"

"An engine caravan—"

"We have no engines," she said, over him. "I think you have no engines, either, but you have the memory of them."

"You don't know," he said. "We have engines. My father has one. I will get to Selareme without your stupid beasts."

She turned to him then, her pale eyes empty.

"It is farther than you think," she said, and walked away from him across the dusty fields to her caravan.

Thes kicked at the pebbles beneath his feet.

She stopped and looked back.

"Are you coming?"

He scuffed at the dirt again for a few seconds before he followed her. The tiny bells on her clothing sang as she walked, and the wind pressed the loose folds against her legs and belly. Thes could not keep his eyes away from the shape of her.

The camp was quiet in the day's heat, and she led him around its skirts to an area behind the tents where the massive dlkii drowsed in the shade.

"Here," she said, and took his hand to place against a beast's warm hide. Thes rubbed his palm across the dlkii's flank, feeling the rough hair and loose skin. Even in the dust, the animals smelled of grass.

"And here," she said, pulling his hand away from the animal's side and pressing it over her breast. She pushed into him, working her leg between his to get closer. He flushed, excited and embarrassed and unsure of where to put his other hand. He bent his head to kiss her but she turned her face away.

"Not that," she said.

Her hands burrowed under his clothes. "Like this," she said, and rocked her hips against him. Thes was too aware of the dlkii's warm breathing behind him, of the sun just beyond the shadows. He shoved her away, at once regretting it. He reached for her, but his fingers only brushed her sleeve as she moved back.

She shook her head and shifted inside her clothing.

"You don't want this? Do you want the other, then?"

He could not tell if she were dismissing him. His fists clenched against his sides.

"Why did you even come here?" he asked sharply. "You don't bring anything but fancy trash, nothing we can even use. Bring engines if you're going to come. Bring tools, or fuel—not all this decoration."

Qarathamlimolo stood back from him. She reached up and smoothed her pale hair, her loose sleeves sliding down her thin brown arms in pools. Beads glittered and clinked under her hands. Her slender fingers worked free any tangles the wind had made. Thes watched her, angry and compelled. She would not look at him. He realized he had brought her to tears.

Thes left her there among the drowsing dlkii, running back to the familiarity of Miridaj's crumbling walls.

***

The Dlsarii would be gone before the rains came and turned the fields to yellow mud. They were packing already, drawing down the banners and folding away any tent not immediately in use. Children gathered to watch them leave as they had to watch them come. Thes watched, too, when he could leave his father's shop. There was a quality of ritual in witnessing the Dlsarii prepare to move on, as if they measured time for Miridaj. Now, the seasons could turn their slow wheel until the Dlsarii came again.

Thes was glad. He wanted to look at the eastern horizon again without seeing the bright tents between him and the mountains. Lim had come to him twice more after he refused her in the tent, but he let her, despite the awkwardness he felt. When she was gone, he could let his fumblings with her fade into the dusty past.

He did not expect her to seek him out again. She was a shadow on the door, and then she was in the shop. She seemed always to know when he was alone there. He did not want to be alone with her, not anymore.

She held out an oblong package wrapped in white cloth. He took it from her, wary of such gifts.

"It's a set of magnets," she said, not waiting for him to unwrap it. Then she reached into a deep pocket in her coat and pulled out a spool of green-crusted wire. She pressed it into his empty hand.

"Copper," she said. "You can use this, can't you?"

He looked at what he held, and his cheeks grew hot.

"We find things like this," she said. "Remnants. From before."

He closed his fingers around the spool. The metal warmed against his skin. When Thes was a child, his father had told him about the fragments of old machines scattered between the cities, and showed him a small, frozen clockwork he had found while digging in the fields.

"This is what you want, isn't it?" she asked.

"Better than beads," he said, putting her gifts down on his workbench. He picked up a chisel and touched it to the spinning grindwheel, shutting her out as she stood there. Her hand lay on the door handle. The wheel whined down into a slow growl as the electricity stuttered and went out. Thes sighed and got out the hand file.

She shrugged, lingering, watching him. "You feed the dlkii and they work. There is no waiting for there to be power."

He stared at her.

"Why haven't you gone already?" he said, stung.

Her mouth twisted down against tears.

"Soon enough," she said, and disappeared out the door. Bright sun slashed across the floor and was erased as the door swung shut behind her.

**

Thes locked the shop door as dusk came down, stood and stretched his cramped shoulders in the still-busy street. His father had left hours ago to tend Thes's mother. The dust was in her lungs. She had been coughing for weeks, it seemed, and was fading. Thes squinted up past the rooftops at the dimming sky. Soon it would rain. It would be better then.

He dawdled. He didn't want to see his mother yet. His thoughts were still on the bag he had begun packing with extra clothes, food, and tools he would want when he left. If he left. He shook his head. When. *When.*

He had drifted aimlessly toward the end of the street when the pack of boys surged past him, and Ems came to a stuttering halt to grab his arm and drag him into it.

"Dlsarii girl," Ems panted. "Doesn't know she's out too late."

"Where?"

"Next street. We split, catch her that way."

Thes joined the hunt, blood in his eyes, thoughts of his leaving left behind.

They ran her down outside the city, in the grey dusty space between their walls and her caravan. If the Dlsarii heard her scream for help, they never answered. The younger boys swarmed over her, too many to fight. She jangled like chimes, her decorated hair and clothing tangled and ripped by too many hands. Dust smeared across her open mouth as she was driven into the ground, her face painted now in mud. Thes was not surprised to see Qarathamlimolo was the prey. She did not have the sense to stay away. At last she stopped fighting, and they did what they would. Thes closed his eyes, straying back from the scuffle. He did not try to stop them.

***

Years slid by under the slow tread of the dlkii before the Dlsarii wound their way back to Miridaj, materializing in the haze of the plains, distilled from the sun. They had crossed many mountain ranges, seen many cities built and rebuilt, passed news among them and traded and intermarried. It was Miridaj's time again. And so they came.

Miridaj had changed very little. Its walls still slumped in places, its streets were still narrow and petered out into the fields. Thes's parents were long dead. The shop was his. He had not prospered, but he had not failed. He had his own wife, his own children who played in the oiled streets and ran in the dust outside the walls. The children were excited and impatient to see the visitors, but Thes had no interest in watching the Dlsarii come into his city again, dressed like legends as they walked through the market. He still had to work to keep out Lim's ghost.

He waited to leave for home until after he judged the Dlsarii had gone back to their tents. The air was blue with nightfall, and a thin wind had sprung up as the day's temperature cooled. He was surprised by a pale-haired boy waiting across the street from his shop. The boy crossed to meet him, staring flatly. Thes looked into a familiar face. This boy looked like Thes's other sons, but with the wash of his mother's coloring. His eyes were light, but not so icy, his skin tawny but not as brown. He must be around fourteen. Nearly grown. Thes put his hand in his pocket around the heavy clutch of keys there. He nodded slowly at the boy, admitting his claim.

"She told me you'd still be here," the boy said. "She said you'd never find an engine."

Thes frowned, a flicker of annoyance staining him.

"What did she name you?" he asked.

"Tevilsheniesdi," the boy said. Remembered music rolled with the word.

"None of mine in that," Thes said, half to himself.

The boy stood silently, as if waiting for Thes to do something. His eyes were veiled. Thes looked down at his hands. They were scarred and cut, the knuckles like knots. A cart rattled by in the cross street, its rough engine spitting fumes into the air. He looked up, over the boy's head.

"Go back to your mother," he said. "There's nothing here for you."

"She's gone on," the boy said.

"To Selareme?"

"Maybe. Maybe to Deskaniej out north. She leads where she wants."

"Well then," said Thes.

Dust gritted in his teeth. The wind filled the air with it, and the mask hung around his neck could not filter it all out even if he wore it. After a while in silence, he went back inside, leaving Lim's son to stay or go as he wished. Thes knew the boy was his. It was plain in his face. He did not need to stand and stare.

Ilis came in a moment behind him. Thes felt the weight of her eyes on him. He glanced up. She was silhouetted against the doorway, her shadowed face rimmed with yellow lamp light.

"I was wondering why you were so late. The boys said you never came home tonight. They said you let them go to the market alone."

He arranged his tools in neat lines on his workbench. "What do you want, Ilis?"

"Tell me how you come to have a Dlsarii son," she said. "Tell me how his mother knew to bring him here, to our doorstep."

"Shut up," he said. "Get out of here."

She leaned against the doorframe, arms crossed tightly at her waist.

"If he stays, he is yours alone. I have enough without raising another woman's child."

Thes flipped the switch for the grindwheel, hoping for electricity. The wheel spun slowly for half a turn before it stopped.

"Get out," he said again, but she had already slid out the door into the gathering night. Thes looked out the door at an empty street. The boy was gone. Thes didn't think he'd see that one again.

***

The mountains stilled crouched on the far horizon like sleeping cats. The night blurred them, but their weight still pressed up against the starry sky. Thes turned his eyes away from them as he finally left the shop. He told himself they were only hills, and that the Dlsarii in their brightly lit tents had lied about the vastness of the world. He did not believe in Selareme.

II.
FAITH

OLDER THINGS

VANDA WAS AT the kitchen sink, rinsing off a bunch of grapes and daydreaming, when she glanced out the window and spotted the fox.

At first she thought it was one of the local feral cats, lying in a neat tuck in the middle of the lawn and watching the birds at the feeder. Then the creature lifted its head and spread its long sharp jaws wide in a yawn, opening a void ringed by black lips and white teeth.

Vanda leaned over the sink for a closer look. The fox caught the motion and stared back at her through the window, its round yellow eyes unreadable. Its directness made her uneasy. She wondered if it might be rabid.

Then the fox yawned again, rose, and trotted off into the messy scrub of the field behind Vanda's yard. She watched the fringe of weeds for any more movement, but the fox was gone.

***

Vanda missed John sometimes. It had been a good enough marriage, even while they were growing apart for the last decade of it. He had been kind. They had been friends. His death had been unexpected, after a very brief illness. She didn't like to admit to herself it had also been a relief, the weeds of widowhood so much easier to navigate than the complexities of divorce.

She had boxed up his belongings and stacked them neatly in the basement. She wasn't ready to get rid of them yet. As much as she relished her new solitude, she was still adjusting to being by herself after twenty years as a couple. She missed another voice in the house, someone to help with the everyday chores. But she couldn't deny it was easier now that John was gone. Her days were entirely her own without him.

After her bereavement leave ended, she arranged to take a leave of absence. She needed time away from the classroom and the politics of the university. She needed *time*.

She looked forward to working in the yard, by herself, for as long as she wanted. She thought it would be good for her. John had never wanted to change the yard, content to let the beds and shrubbery become shaggy and overgrown.

Privacy, he called the unchecked growth. The high yew hedges meant no one could see what they did.

***

Oaks dotted the property, old trees left standing by the developers when the houses were first built. Their tall crowns softened the sunlight, keeping her yard in shade. Moss spread through the grass, and her fading flower garden straggled from its bed in search of stronger light.

The lots were deep but narrow, and she was used to hearing the background noises of suburbia around her. She hadn't realized how quiet the neighborhood was during the day, with people away at work. Her house was isolated at the street's end, at the back of the development, far off from the traffic on the main road. She stood in the stillness of her yard, drinking in the peace of being alone.

Fortified, she opened the garage and dragged out her tools. She wanted to start with the stand of elderberry dying beside the porch door. Only a few sagging branches had produced any fruit this year, and the birds had picked them clean long ago. The spot was too shady and dry for elderberry. The shrub had been ailing since they bought the house six years before, and Vanda was mildly surprised it had lasted this long. She thought if she could move it, it might survive a while longer.

***

The ground around the elderberry was soft with years of decaying leaves, and when she raked them up the sweet tobacco smell of them filled the cool air. She bent down, her mouth open to taste the scent.

As she dug her hands into the leaf pile to scoop the litter up, something stabbed through her glove into the base of her middle finger. She swore and stood up, expecting to see a broken stick jammed into her hand. Instead, she saw a square black nail head. She pulled it out, surprised at how deep it had gone, and tugged off the torn glove.

Bright drops of blood spattered on the leaves at her feet as she assessed the damage. The wound burned, but the blood helped wash it clean. She pulled a tissue from her pocket and pressed it hard against the puncture. She was glad she was up to date on her tetanus booster.

She held onto the nail and went inside to take care of her hand.

***

The peroxide foamed and stung, washing away flecks of leaf and drying blood. When she had bandaged her wound, she turned her attention to the cause of it.

The nail puzzled her. It wasn't rusted. The metal was almost greasy in its smoothness. But its shape, the square head, the squared shank, made her think it was old. Colonial, possibly, or at least handmade. The development was put up in the 1940s, part of the postwar housing boom. But there had been something here before. And before that, too, she was sure. History didn't start with the colonies. She turned the nail over in her uninjured hand, wondering how long it had been in the ground.

Unsatisfied, she set it on the kitchen windowsill as a curiosity. She would look into it, she thought, eventually.

***

The upstairs rooms gave a different view of her yard that was always a subtle surprise. The work she had done in the yard seemed somehow far less from above. Her lot backed to undeveloped land, separated by a tidy fieldstone wall from wet fields and patchy woods surrounding the curving dead end street, a few dozen empty acres until the next development started.

Deer were frequent visitors, and cats both feral and stray. Hawks hunted there.

She saw a pair of foxes, too, every few days, skirting the edge of her yard, hunting mice, basking in pools of autumn sun. It looked to her like a mother and kit. Sometimes they sat and stared at the house. She knew they were aware of her. She imagined they studied her, learning what they could of her alien ways. She studied them in return. The larger fox had a damaged front paw. Vanda thought it had lost a toe.

***

Vanda could not get comfortable. The bed was too big around her, and her hand ached, breaking into the depths of her sleep, pushing her toward a strange twilight. She dreamed of the dull, distracting pain. She dreamed of the foxes, and of other things that were not foxes. She dreamed of her injured paw, and running, and running.

***

When the puncture had begun to close, Vanda returned to her work in the yard.

She scraped through the leaf litter at the base of the elderberry again and found two more iron nails driven in among the roots.

"Someone believed in witches," she said aloud to herself. She hadn't realized how clearly she remembered her grandmother's superstitions.

She pried the nails out of the ground, disliking the feel of them. They looked just like the first one, squared off and too clean.

She got up to put them in the coffee can of nails and screws she kept in the garage. She didn't want them near her.

***

With the sharp blade of the spade, she cut into the mat of shallow roots still binding the shrub to the ground. They gave way with snaps that sounded like tight strings breaking. As she pulled the woody stalks free, a scattering of pale objects fell from beneath them, no longer held fast among the roots. Vanda placed the elderberry safely on a tarp and knelt to see.

She picked the yellowed fragments from the loose soil and rolled them across her palm, raising them up toward the light. They were bones of some sort, small and straight and unidentifiable. She closed her hand around them, filled with a sudden sorrow. Something had died here, forgotten and lost.

She placed the bones gently back in the disturbed earth and covered them again.

As she stood, she wiped her eyes with the back of her wrist. She didn't know why the bones bothered her so much, or how they even could. She swallowed down tears and dragged the elderberry toward the back of the house.

***

Worn out from an entire day in the yard, she turned out the downstairs lights before eight and looked from the back windows at the moonlit yard. She didn't see the foxes among the moving shadows, but she was sure they were out there, watching her. She pulled the curtains shut against the night and climbed the stairs to bed.

***

The creature's hot breath stirred the hair on her neck. She smelled dust and dry grass and the tang of animal feces. It was a fox, and it was not a fox. It circled her and leaned in, its muzzle almost against her skin. Vanda shuddered. It was taller than she was and thin as a lash, all muscle beneath its shining amber skin, with a mane of black hair, and eyes of sharp gold locked onto hers. In the yard, a smaller creature, the tall one's mirror, sniffed at the rock wall and at the bases of trees, and pissed over whatever scent it found there. Marking. Laying claim.

Vanda raised her hand to fend the tall fox away and barely felt its long, needle teeth as they sank into the meat of her palm. But she screamed when it tore the meat free.

She opened her eyes, suddenly, shockingly awake. Her hand was balled into a tight fist, her nails dug in, ripping the skin. She forced her hand open and reached for the light. Even in the safety of the yellow glow, her heart beat too hard. She breathed deeply, trying to calm herself.

She wished John were still with her, to keep her imagination at bay.

***

Unrested, Vanda forced herself out of bed and to the kitchen for coffee, for breakfast, for a better start to the day. She did not want to go back to sleep and lose the new routine of her life. She needed that rhythm, or she feared she would fall apart.

She gazed at the yard, the fields, sipping at her too-hot coffee. Mist crept among the grasses and trees, not yet burnt away by the weak rising sun. The foxes, mother and kit, sat and watched her from the top of the rock wall, their long tails wrapped around their black legs.

She rubbed her tired eyes and blinked.

They were not foxes. Not entirely. She had dreamed these creatures.

As she watched, afraid to move, to startle them, the larger fox sidled up to the house and stood upright on impossibly long legs to look in the window. Only the thin glass kept it outside. It pressed its nose to the glass, panting to find a scent. Its face wrinkled against something pungent. It backed away, then dropped below the window's frame. Vanda heard its claws clicking on the deck, exploring.

She knew the screened porch door was locked, and the kitchen door too, but she held her breath until she saw the fox cross the yard again and disappear with the small one into the fields.

***

The mist lingered and the day stayed grey, with a fine, spitting rain falling at intervals. Vanda stayed in, tired and on edge. She wandered through her house like a stranger, realizing how much she had put away of her own life when she packed up John's. She peered out the windows, expecting to see the foxes again. The yard remained empty under the wet sky. She could see the elderberry listing in its new bed, but could not bring herself to go out and stake it. She retreated to the dull space of the living room and lay on the couch with a fleece throw over her legs.

When her phone rang, she let it go to voicemail.

"Hey, Vand," her sister said into her ear when she played the message. "Just checking in since you didn't call me this week. If you want me to come over and help with anything, just call me. Or just call me. Okay? Okay. I'll talk to you soon."

Vanda deleted the message.

Perhaps it was exhaustion, or unadmitted grief. Perhaps it was only the mist and her imagination. She was not frightened by the foxes as she dreamed them. She wanted them to be real. She wanted something extraordinary to end the emptiness that had curled itself around her.

***

Vanda was slow to separate the click of claws on the deck from the patter of rain and falling acorns. She put down the book on local history she was browsing and went to the kitchen. In the fading afternoon light, she could see the tall fox pacing back and forth across the deck on its hind legs, its head scanning from side to side, seeking. When it saw her, it came toward the window, sniffing, reaching for her, but as many times as it drew close, it retreated, repelled.

Vanda followed its gaze to the iron nail still resting on the sill. She put her hand over it. The fox watched her intently, glancing between Vanda's face and her bandaged hand. Vanda picked the nail up gingerly, cringing at the uncomfortable cold against her skin. She dropped it into the garbage. When she turned back to the window, the fox was gone.

She stood silent, listening. She thought she could hear it, stealthy, moving along the side of the house. She moved toward the kitchen door at the sound of something scraping on the siding.

Then came the snick and creak of the porch's screen door opening, and the scratch of long claws on tile.

Vanda froze. Her breath hitched in her throat as she whispered a prayer, willing magic.

She opened the door.

The fox stepped from the porch into the kitchen, tense and wary as the wild thing it was.

Vanda held still so as not to frighten it away, and drank in the sight of it. Its fine red fur, speckled with coppery strands. Its hot golden eyes. Its black hands, black feet, black tongue, and white, white teeth. It came close, and she could smell its scent of musk and dry leaves. It circled her, and she watched the bones of its spine roll beneath its skin like a string of beads, sinuous, strong.

It sniffed at her, then reached out tentatively with a long, paw-like hand to stroke her uncombed hair. It was missing a finger.

Vanda swallowed the urge to speak to it. Instead, she raised her own damaged hand in an echo of the creature's movements. It bent its head slowly to meet her gesture, and opened its jaws.

The wet crunch of bones as its bite crushed her hand seemed as distant as the moon. Vanda winced at the hard tug as the creature worked her finger loose. She gasped in surprise, but the pain was blunt and far away. She drew her arm back. Blood flowed from the rough stump where her finger had been, and dripped from the fox's lips. It chewed. It swallowed. It pushed its wet snout into Vanda's face, nuzzled her, marked her, breathed its hot red breath over her.

Vanda reached up again and this time ran her bleeding hand over its smooth fur, over the long black mane, smearing it as it smeared her. The fox snarled and moved back.

Vanda stood still and murmured to it that it was okay, that she wouldn't hurt it, that she only wanted to know it was real.

It turned away from her and slunk from the confines of the house.

Vanda grabbed a dishtowel and wrapped it tightly around her hand. She could see the fox already at the edge of her yard, fast on two long legs. The smaller fox darted in and out of the tall grass, whining and restless. In the right light, they might still be just foxes. But she could see they were not.

She watched them from the porch, unsure of what she should do. Blood seeped through the dishtowel, but her hand didn't hurt anymore. She dropped the cloth and held up her hand. The stump had begun to scar over.

The tall fox looked back at her and let out a string of high yips.

They were waiting.

Vanda left the screen door to flap open behind her as she went into the yard. The foxes shivered at the sound of her boots on the deck. She kicked them off and stepped barefoot into the leaf-scattered grass.

The yard seemed so small now, bounded by houses and dying flower beds. As she loped across it, the creatures moved away, leading her toward the wide wild space, going slowly enough that she could catch up.

When Vanda reached the rock wall, she paused, shucked her jeans, and squatted, marking the stones with her piss. Then she followed the foxes up into the field, toward the trees.

SEVEN STARS

SEVEN STARS IN the Empress's crown.

Paul blinked, surprised by the clarity of the memory.

Alice had sung that single phrase to Paul one night as they sat on their haunches at the back of his parents' yard, stoned and gazing up at the black shape of the hill in the middle distance. Her voice was flat, and the words didn't fit the tune, but she repeated them until she got bored with the sound of herself. Alice had started calling the hill the Empress sometime over the summer. No one else Paul knew called it anything but the hill.

It didn't really need a name. Everyone knew what it was.

Paul pushed down thoughts of Alice and her song, forcing his attention to the present, even as he gazed across the empty fields to where the hill still loomed. It was autumn and unnervingly hot, with no motion to stir the heavy air as the afternoon wound down. Stan handed him a beer, then settled into his green plastic lawn chair. Paul looked around slowly, taking in the once-familiar neighborhood. The changes he saw superimposed themselves on his clear memory.

***

The six houses on the cul-de-sac were all split-levels, put up in the late sixties. Their yards backed to scrubby wasteland that had endured through numerous waves of development, the terrain too rough to bother with. Paul had grown up on the cul-de-sac and played back there in the fields when he was a kid. He had moved away after college, and his parents had sold the house and moved south.

Between the two houses on the right of the street's curve, a thin path ran back through the fields and into the cover of sparse, scattered trees. He was surprised to see it.

"We wore that trail in the grass going back there as kids," Paul said.

Stan sipped his beer. Unlike Paul, he had not moved away. He still lived in his parents' old place, the first house on the right. That house at least hadn't changed. It showed its age in its faded siding and white brick. "I remember. I still see kids using it now and then. Teenagers."

"Do they still go all the way out to the hill?"

Stan nodded. "I would think they do."

As if on cue, three kids, two girls and a boy, trailed out of the scrub and grass to cut across the corner of the lawn, following the old path. They kept their heads down, walking in single file, in step with each other. They paid no attention to Stan and Paul as they passed by. Paul could see the dust stuck to their skin and to their jeans, see how their hair was matted with it. Moths, disturbed by their passage, fluttered up from the grass.

Paul turned his head to watch them as they made their way out to the street.

"They can't be more than thirteen or fourteen," he said. "They go like they know what they're doing."

Stan half-smiled, not showing any teeth. "Of course they do. Don't you remember how much we knew when we were their age?"

Paul laughed and wiped the cool, sweating beer can across his forehead before he opened it. "This heat," he said.

The air was like midsummer, thickly humid. The night would come down soon, but the October days were too short to carry such heat. There was a strangeness to it, the heat and the light out of balance.

"It's filthy," Stan said. "I've been seeing birds just lying dead on the ground, like they couldn't take it and fell while they flew. Sparrows, mostly. Too small to handle it."

Paul sipped his beer. "It doesn't feel like it's been twenty-six years," he said. "Feels like we're still just waiting for our ride to a concert."

Stan shook his head, looking out toward the hill again. It had turned a deep blue in the changing light.

"So, what really brought you back?" Stan finally asked.

Paul exhaled.

"The divorce was harder than I thought it would be," he said. "After Cynthia left, I just really wanted to come home. It was time."

"That's tough," Stan said. "Look, do you want to stay for dinner? I was going to make spaghetti."

"Raincheck," Paul said, standing. "I have to unpack some stuff so I can function. The apartment is a lot smaller than I thought it would be."

"Okay then," Stan said. "You know where to find me."

***

It was several days before Paul drifted back to visit Stan. He picked up a couple of sandwiches after work and brought them over for a cold dinner. The sky was already shifting from gold to blue as he pulled into Stan's driveway.

Stan still had his plastic chairs facing the fields. The holes worn in the lawn showed how long they'd been there.

"Look around," Stan said, mid-thought, as Paul took a seat beside him. "We're in a hollow, as wide as it is. Three or four miles wide. Probably a crater of some sort. Meteorite strike. The hill is at its center."

"Okay," Paul said, proffering the bag. "Are you hungry? There's ham and cheese or turkey."

"Do you have any idea how old that hill is?" Stan said, flicking the bright butt of his cigarette into the darkening sky to punctuate his question.

"Old," Paul said.

Stan glanced sideways at him. "It's younger than you think, even though its eroded, with the rock all worn away at the top and shoulders. In daylight you can see how the rock is twisted and folded too, and how the folds are worn down. That rock is sedimentary, I think. Easier to wear away."

He paused to tap a fresh cigarette from his dwindling pack, gesturing with it without lighting it.

"But you can also see the dark rock that pushed into it. That's not from around here. I don't know how it got here. Moving through the earth somehow. Or falling out of the sky."

Paul nodded in acknowledgement.

"But what's really worth noticing is how that hill stands alone. Look around. Nothing like it until the mountain ring starts up, what, eight or ten miles away?"

He motioned to the south, where the mountains did indeed stand against the sky.

"That's not how mountains should form," Stan said. "Not with outliers like this hill."

Paul nodded again, not sure where Stan was leading.

"It's lonely," Stan said. He put the cigarette back in the pack and took the bag of sandwiches from Paul.

"Let's go inside. I gave up and put the air back on."

Stan was quiet while they ate, and Paul let his attempts at small talk drift into silence. But as they finished, Stan again began speaking from the middle of his own thoughts.

"And it's weird, but I don't think the kids know why they want to come up here. I know I didn't, not in a way I could understand enough to explain. But it seemed—appropriate, somehow. Not right, but...right."

Paul balled up the waxed paper sandwich wrappings and stuffed them into the bag.

"Do you ever go up there anymore?" he asked.

"No. Not for years," Stan said. "Of course, I still feel the urge. But I can't just go running through other people's back yards anymore."

***

The heat would not let go. Every time Paul returned to the cul-de-sac, the heat and the landscape dragged him back to that summer with Alice. He had enough in his life to mourn without adding her.

The last time he had come over, Stan had made chicken salad for them. Tonight, Paul brought burgers. He and Stan had established their pattern and were well on their way to a rut. The divorce had been chaos. A familiar pattern was what Paul needed now.

"I always thought I missed my father," Stan said without preamble as Paul sat down. He drew on his cigarette, blew the smoke up to the darkening sky. "I didn't realize until later that it was the idea of him I missed. Shit, I was sixteen when he died. I didn't even know him."

He threw the butt of the cigarette out onto the lawn. It glowed there like a red firefly.

"I miss my mom though," Stan added.

Paul kept his eyes on the dark hill crouched behind the trees, already black against the deepening blue sky. "Yeah, well," he said, and stopped. His parents were alive. He had no frame of reference. He didn't want to sound dismissive with an empty comment.

"It was after my dad died that I really felt the pull of the hill. I guess the idea of community, of communion, with the other kids who went up filled in the empty space where my family used to be." Stan paused, flicked his lighter a couple of times, making sparks without flame.

"You would think that there would still be a family, even with one part missing. But there wasn't. My mother wasn't strong enough to hold us together. She didn't understand my sister at all, and Ellen took off as soon as she graduated."

Stan sighed.

"And you know what happened with me."

"Yeah, well," Paul said again. Those had been ugly years, and he had moved away before Stan outgrew them.

Stan turned to face Paul. It had grown too dark to read his expression with any certainty.

"That hill calls to kids because kids don't know how to fill the holes in their lives. They don't know how to live with parts missing. Not enough experience. What's up there, it offers them something."

Paul realized how tight his grip had become on the smooth plastic arms of his chair.

"You're starting to sound a little like me now," Paul said.

Stan snorted. "Sorry."

They sat in silence for a while, watching the stars come out.

***

Another part of the familiar pattern was the daily pilgrimage. The kids came trooping down as the sun sank, heading home to dinner. As usual, they ignored Stan and Paul as they trespassed.

But Paul swiveled to watch them until they reached the sidewalk and dispersed into the hot golden light. He rose and looked back up the trail.

"Stan," he said. "One of the girls didn't come down."

"You're right," Stan said after a minute, keeping his eyes on the fields.

Paul took a step toward the path. Stan sighed, and stood, and stretched.

"Let me get my walking stick."

The dusty trail snaked back past the clipped edges of the yards, down through the brush that filled the low, wide basin. The ground sloped away subtly, not enough to make the walk difficult but enough to take them out of view from the surrounding houses. Even though they had only travelled a few hundred feet, the sense of isolation was heavy.

"We don't have a lot of time tonight," Stan said.

"I know," Paul said. "But we have to at least see."

The trail brought them out to the edge of a pond that filled a smooth oval depression in the wider basin. Scrub willows grew around it, shaggy and split by lightning. Rocks the size of melons had been placed around the pond in an uneven border. Cans and jars were set into nooks in the rocks and into the crooks of the trees. The containers were full of water, and dusted with a murky film of yellow pollen.

"I don't remember this," Paul said.

"Nor I," said Stan. "But we've been gone a long time. Rituals change."

The trail continued through the sparse grass on the other side of the pond, winding around regularly spaced piles of rocks like a maze. Shadows swelled to fill the wide hollow, the air turning lavender around them although the sky above still held its brightness. The hill was a stronger presence here, in the quiet. Its shoulders seemed to shrug up, to bear the weight of the stars above them. There was a sense of dry awareness in the mass of rock, as if it listened without caring what noises the chattering humans made to it. As if it chose to ignore them.

"I just want to see what they've done with the rocks, and then we go," Paul said. "I don't like it here."

Stan nodded. "Do you feel the pull of it?"

Paul shook his head. Their voices seemed too loud here. As if their own noises covered the sounds of something else.

They followed the trail a few yards farther, into the midst of the rock piles. The piles wound into a broad spiral. Between them the ground was scraped clear of vegetation, down to its brown dust. A long shape stretched on the bare space near the center.

"Oh," Stan said softly, caught off guard. He had recognized it.

A girl lay on the ground as if she had been dropped from the sky, blanketed in dust, no part of her skin or clothing clean. Moths clung in her hair like bits of paper confetti. Like lost souls, Paul thought as he went to her and knelt beside her in the gathering dusk. White wings fluttered at his approach. There are so many, he thought. So many.

He reached out to turn her over, but stopped himself before he touched her. He watched, but did not see her breathing. He stood up.

"Stan?" he said.

Stan came closer to prod at the girl's hip with his walking stick, and screamed when she crumbled like ash under the slight pressure. The moths scattered.

"She's not real," Paul said, frightened wonder in his voice. "She's a sand sculpture. How did they make her? How did they do it?"

Stan took Paul's arm and steered him away. A dry wind picked up, kicking up the dust behind them.

Paul let himself be led. But after a few steps he turned, sure that he saw someone following. A plume of dust rose in the air like a dancer in veils. A human shape hung like a ghost inside. The wind swept it closer.

"Stan," he said, pulling Stan around to look.

Stan started, then swung his stick through the cloud, dispersing it.

"We have to go. Now," he said, and broke into an awkward run.

Paul ran with him through the failing light, to the safety of pavement and suburbia.

***

Paul stayed home the next night, restless, his nerves over-sensitive. The strange, still night was again too warm for this late in autumn. He wondered how long until the heat wave broke. The early nightfall made him too aware of the discordance. Sounds of life going on in the other apartments only emphasized the disarray in his.

The apartment building quieted as the night wore down. He went to bed but sleep escaped him. Alice filled its place, with her sing-song refrain of the seven stars in the Empress's crown. The rhythm of her song merged with the stuttering rhythm of what else she had whispered to him that summer. What her father did to her when she was small. How she worried about her sister. When Paul closed his eyes, Alice looked like the girl made of dust. What was he supposed to have done? He turned the ceiling fan to the highest setting and wrestled with the sweaty sheets. Coming back here had been no answer.

Near dawn, the wind rose to a gale, and a storm crashed through with a pressure like the threat of a tornado in its wake. Branches snapped in the garden behind the building. Rain fell with the weight of stones on the roof. Paul, still awake, welcomed the new rhythm that drove out the old. Alice's voice couldn't sing over this.

The downpour ended with daybreak, but left the sky a hazy, dim yellow and the air reloaded with humidity. Paul finally slept when the sun rose, its autumn angle filling his room with gold.

When he woke, the shadows were creeping in. After the shadows would come the stars, he thought. Seven stars in the Empress's crown.

***

The next time Paul went to the cul-de-sac, Stan had moved his chairs up to the patio, away from the verge. Stan stood when Paul came around the side of the house.

"How are you?" he said, meaning it.

"I have to go up," Paul said. "It's in my head. I have to see what's up there and put it to rest."

Stan shook his head. "Okay," he said. "I understand that. But I'm not going with you."

"I don't expect you to," Paul said. He smiled, but it was a mask.

Stan shrugged.

"It's late to start," he said, and sat down again in his familiar vigil. "I'll be here when you come back down."

Paul nodded and crossed the lawn, passed over the border into the wild scrub. Dust floated up around his feet as he went. Moths scattered. He felt the pull of it, harder now that he was alone, out of sight of the houses. Long shadows stretched out from the thin trees and clumps of grass.

He reached the pool with its rusted votive offerings. The water rippled under a breeze, but it was not enough to clear the caul of dust that covered it. He kept his distance as he passed it, and picked up the path again on its other side.

The area described by the piled rocks was empty now, just a circle of dust. Paul walked into it, tentative, and stopped at what he judged was the center. He turned until he faced the hill. From where he stood in the pattern, it looked as if the high knob of stone wore a crown of stars, dim against the fading sky. He did not count them. He knew their number.

He pushed on. It wasn't far to the hill now. The trail widened as it angled gradually upward. Paul's breath came more quickly, and he realized he was climbing the hill's skirts. Dusk filled in the hollow below him. He climbed toward what was left of the light.

The wind picked up as the sun fell. It was still too warm. It seemed even warmer on the hill. The light was deep amber, slipping fast toward blue. Paul figured it was near six now, and it would be full dark in less than half an hour. He stopped climbing to let the wind dry the sweat on his face.

He leaned against an outcropping and looked over the sloped shoulder of the hill as it bent away before him. He was higher than he expected, almost at the summit. The bowl of earth stretched away, limited at last by a ring of electric light where it met the surrounding streets. As he rested, he looked around, thinking of how Stan had described it, matching it to what he saw.

Where the native rock had weathered away, it revealed deep folds and curves where it had bent under steady downward pressure. Intrusions of dark, alien rock nestled into the hilltop among the folds like eyes in sockets, warping the rock below it. Even under the scattered dust it was glossy, threaded with deep red and green veins and occasional streaks of dull yellow. When Paul brushed it clean, it gleamed opalescent. But the feel of it was uncomfortable under his palm, warm, almost like flesh, and still as ungiving as stone. He took his hand away and stood free of it. He glanced up at the sky. It was time to go back.

As he turned, a different sheen caught his eye. There, in the dark rock, he could make out the arch of an eye socket, the curve of a skull. Dull minerals traced the line of mandible. Paul bent and looked further, brushing away loose soil to find the scroll of a collarbone, broken but still in place. He stood, wiped his face with dusty hands, looked again from his new angle. In the heavy, fading light, the shapes could be intrusions of quartz into the older black rock. They had to be. The rock could not have absorbed bones whole.

He looked around him and saw that where the rocks were scrubbed clean by wind there were many more suggestively skeletal shapes trapped like flies in amber. Was one of them Alice, he thought, caught in final devotion to her Empress? He could picture her as she had been at sixteen, kneeling in some ritual, her brown hair tangled against her neck, grey eyes lifted up to count the stars as the black stone crept its way over her legs and hips and upraised arms until the hill had swallowed her whole and her bones floated in the dark matrix.

"Seven stars," he said without thinking, following the old cadence of her song. It was the comfort of old memory, of youth and unquestioned faith. He repeated it. And again.

And she answered.

She twisted in the black rock with a sound like the grinding of sand on stone, eroding her way free. Basalt had filled the hollows where rich marrow had been, cracking the bones with its weight. Still, she pulled her broken spine upright, balanced her stony skull upon it with ponderous care. She turned her barren face to him, and the stars ranged behind her in a circlet.

He screamed as mindlessly as he had sung out. In a panic he fell and rolled down the long slope of the hill, out of the last warmth of dying sunset and into deep shadow. He got his feet under him and stumbled through the dark empty brush for the white pinpricks of manmade light.

***

Stan met him in the middle distance between his yard and the waste land, walking out into the long grass. In the darkness, Paul recognized him by the flare of his cigarette above the sharp glare of his flashlight. Stan threw the light over Paul's face, blinding him and forcing him to stop.

"You okay?" Stan said. His voice trembled.

Paul rasped out an ugly laugh. "Not really."

Stan exhaled. Smoke twisted in the beam of light he held. Paul waited, catching his breath. The warm, strange air was no refreshment.

"You know," Paul started. His voice dropped away. His shoulders sagged. Stan took a step toward him, but Paul waved him off.

"You know," he started again. "You were right about missing the idea of someone. Of not really knowing them but wishing you did."

Paul started walking slowly toward the back yard, as if he were ancient. Stan kept pace with him.

"Do you remember Alice?" Paul said.

Stan stopped. "Alice. Murphy. Yeah. Her family moved away before senior year."

Paul caught up to Stan.

"She isn't what I remembered."

Stan stared at him, swinging the light back up into Paul's face. Paul squinted and looked away, back toward the distant hill.

"We're too old for this," Stan said at last, pointing the flashlight down so Paul could see again. "We've forgotten too much."

Paul lifted his hands helplessly and let them drop.

"Come on," Stan said, turning away with the light and leaving Paul standing with the huge darkness behind him. He hoped he would follow.

Spring, Awakening

"COME ON, MEGGY," Tara said. "It'll be gone if you don't hurry up."

Meggy grew quiet as Tara led her deeper into the woods than she had ever been. Last year's dead leaves crackled underfoot, and budding twigs snatched at their clothes as they pushed through. The ground sloped gently down toward the distant river. Soon their neighborhood was out of sight behind the trees and the rise of the land.

The farther into the woods they went, the more tightly Meggy held onto her sister. Tara grew angry and pulled her hand out of Meggy's.

"I thought you weren't a baby anymore," she said.

"I'm not," Meggy protested.

"Then if you want to see it, you've got to stop acting like one," Tara said, a bite in her words. "There's nothing scary. It's just the woods. They've always been here."

Meggy began to sniffle, and wiped at her eyes with the hem of her shirt.

"What's the matter with you?" Tara said sharply. "You said you wanted to see what I'm doing out here. Now's your chance."

Meggy nodded and followed.

***

After school, Tara headed past her house and into the nature reserve, trudging along the washed-out path until she reached a certain boulder she used as a landmark. From there, she stepped off the marked trail and kept walking. The landscape was still all brown and grey this early in spring. The last of the snow had melted away a few days ago, leaving the ground soft and muddy and riddled with the tracks of deer and smaller creatures. Tara imagined herself tracking them through an unmapped wilderness like the reserve had been once.

Surrounded by cities, these woods preserved the memory of what had been before the cities were built. Horse trails cut through the outer edges, but farther down among the weathered masses of rock that had once been mountains there were far fewer signs of human passage. It was a sudden thing, the abrupt absence of the noise of civilization. As many times as Tara walked down into the depths of the woods, she could never catch the moment that the connection was cut.

Growing up on the edge of the reserve had given her childhood a certain mystique. Her mother had warned her about going too far into the woods alone, and her friends talked about the monsters and killers that hid among the trees, waiting to strike the unwary. Tara sometimes still thought about the dangers, but they were as distant as fairy tales.

Away from her mother and her friends, alone, Tara could be in control of her own fate. She imagined herself a sorceress, a queen, an ageless fey woman, unafraid and with the power of the world at her disposal.

At home, she had to watch her sister, and start dinner, and do the housework her mother didn't have time to do. She wanted to be free of that, free of the responsibilities and expectations put upon her. She wasn't sure of what exactly she wanted, only that she should be able to decide what it was for herself and be able to make it happen without the burden of other people's demands.

She stopped at a broken tree that caught her attention. The tree had cracked in a way that gave it the suggestion of a face, with a hollow in it hanging open like an empty mouth. The small clearing around it was marked with an uneven ring of stones, mossy and half-covered in years of fallen leaves. She knew someone else had found this spot, knew she wasn't the only one who wandered off the paths. Tara looked around for old beer cans and cigarette butts, or any other sign that anyone else had lingered here. There was nothing. Only the broken stump, and the rustling woods around it.

She wondered if anyone else had seen the stump the way she did. She felt a sort of presence there, as if something were waiting to be revealed.

She moved closer, slow, as if something might reach for her. A scattering of small bones lay among the stump's knotted roots. She saw a piece of a jay's wing, and the sharp-toothed skull of a squirrel or chipmunk. It looked like they had been dropped there, like they had fallen out of the hole in the broken tree. She pushed the bones around with the toe of her sneaker, burying them in the leaf litter.

She was suddenly aware of how alone she was, and how far down the sky the sun had fallen. She backed away until she was far enough away to turn and run for home.

***

Tara lay in her bed, in the dark, watching the bright digital numbers of her clock count the minutes. She listened for her mother to come up and go to sleep so she could sneak downstairs to watch videos she couldn't watch when Meggy was around.

And Meggy was always around, asking Tara to play with her, asking Tara where she was going and what she was doing, and why she couldn't come too.

It had been better before Meggy was born. Tara's father had still been around then. He took her for ice cream, and to the park, and let her watch the Saturday morning cartoons her mother couldn't stand. Now she had Meggy but no dad, and her mother had two jobs and worked all the time. She wondered if her dad would still be here if they hadn't had Meggy to try to fix things.

***

A few days later, Tara went back to the clearing. She wanted to feel that presence again.

Already, hints of green had pushed through the remains of last year's growth. The air was still cold, but spring would come, regardless.

People used to worship nature, Tara knew. She'd read about it in mythologies and folklores. The Green Man, Pan, Dionysus, and so many more. People looked to the power behind the cycle of the seasons. They made sacrifices and begged for good harvests. They prayed to the trees.

She could do that. She could figure out how.

She had brought a round, white stone with her that she had found at the beach years ago. She remembered showing it to her dad. He had said it was pretty.

Tara placed the smooth stone in the hollow of the broken stump and stepped back. She clasped her hands, fidgeting and uncertain of what else to do.

The stone didn't seem enough of an offering.

Please, she thought, *please*.

Nothing answered her, no voice, no sense of another consciousness. The absence was enormous. She shivered. She wanted, and she wanted to be heard.

She cobbled together a prayer from her childhood memories, when God was an old man and his son was her friend. *Please*, she begged.

She waited, hoping, but nothing came. Prayers were no use. She wondered what kind of offering would get its attention. It should be something of value, she thought, and the stone had value to her. But it meant nothing to what she hoped to reach.

Inspiration struck her.

Dead leaves crackled under her knees as she crouched close to the hole in the stump and exhaled into it, filling the damp space with her own warm breath. She wanted to feel the hollow draw it in, using it to fill its own indescribable lungs.

Again, she waited. Again, nothing answered. *It wants life,* she thought. *It wants all of it.*

She rummaged around at the base of the stump for anything alive until a swarm of insects scurried away from her. She pinched a beetle from the leaf litter on the ground and shoved it into the hollow as well. She felt the soft wood inside crumble around her fingers as she crushed the beetle against the stone. She wiped her hand on her jeans.

That's better, she thought. *That was a real sacrifice.*

The woods around her went suddenly silent, without birdcall, without the scuttle of small things, without the susurrus of old, moving leaves. Tara froze, too aware of the absence.

In a moment, life resumed.

Tara knew she had gotten something's attention.

***

Many creatures die, their countless lives snuffed out over the single moment of countless years. But this death was something it had not tasted yet, or for ages. The newness of it sparked memory. This death carried intent. Desire and intent.

It was a small thing, full of promise.

It was the seed.

***

When the teacher collected the class's English homework the next day, Tara shrugged when asked for her paper.

"I didn't finish it," she said, testing.

Her teacher blinked as if there were dust in his eyes.

"Okay," he said, and moved on to the next desk. She watched him finish gathering the assignments and return to his desk.

"Today we're starting Chapter 5," he said, his voice flat. The room filled with the sound of textbooks opening.

Tara looked around, but the rest of the class didn't seem to notice that she had gotten away with anything. She yawned and smiled to herself as she opened her book.

She wanted more.

***

She left the house before her mother and Meggy got up. She snuck along the side away from their bedroom windows to where she had made a trap and hidden it in the hedge that enclosed the yard. She was surprised to find she had caught a rabbit. The animal hunched like a rock, frozen, its eyes wide and panicked. She hadn't expected such quick success.

Her breath was a mist on the air as she clutched the trap to her chest and carried it into the reserve. No one else was on the trails as she wound her way in to where the stump waited. A haze of green had emerged over the woods as new growth began to push through. Tara took it as a good sign. Maybe this place hadn't spoken to anyone else. Maybe it had waited for someone to see it as it was, someone who understood what it wanted. She drew in a deep breath of the damp, sweet air. Tara let herself think it had waited for her.

She was a mass of nerves as she considered what she was about to do. She set the trap down and took a deep breath to calm herself, forcing herself to focus on what she wanted from this.

When she unlatched the trap, the rabbit leapt for the opening, but she was ready for it. She held it tightly and pulled it free.

She'd decided on a rabbit because they were so timid and soft. But the rabbit squirmed, trying to find purchase with its strong back legs, scratching her through her shirt until she held it away. It shrieked like a siren. It was stronger than she had expected.

Tara swallowed against the bile rising in her throat, and with a jerk of her wrist twisted the rabbit's head around. The sharp sound of its neck snapping almost made her scream. Its legs still twitched. Even dead, it wanted to escape. She thrust the warm body down into the stump's hollow and waited for what gift would come.

***

"Tara, do the dishes now," her mother said as she finished packing tomorrow's lunches.

Tara looked up from her math homework.

"I don't want to," she said.

Her mother blinked three times, her expression pained, then opened the refrigerator to put the sandwiches away. She closed the door and went to the foot of the stairs.

"Meggy," she called up. "Come do the dishes."

***

Tara lay awake until dawn, still nauseous with excitement, still thinking about how easy it had been to get her way. She was connected to something with real power, and she could use it. But it had to be fed.

***

She cut school the next day, even though she'd done her homework this time. She had seen what she could do, and figured out what it would cost her. She had plans now. But there wasn't enough energy left in her for what she wanted. She would have to find a worthy sacrifice to earn more.

The woods seemed even greener as she ran through them to the broken stump, with its small, dark hollow and its promise.

Just being in the wild space made her feel stronger, alive with other selves, other instincts. She sat in the mud before the stump, absorbing its presence. It knew who she was. She was sure of it.

The clearing was quiet around her. Birds called and flittered at a distance. No small things scratched at the old fallen leaves or damp ground. The insects had moved on. Tara closed her eyes and let the noises and scents of the place fill her. Something here had to be good enough as a tribute to the thing she worshipped to get her what she desired.

Worship, she thought. *That's what this is. That's what I'm doing. How weird.*

Whatever it was she had found was older than she could imagine, she knew, and any name she gave it now would be meaningless and forgotten in the blink of an eye.

She closed her eyes and let her mind wander, until a spark of inspiration flared.

She opened her eyes and crawled to the stump, rising onto her knees to reach the hollow heart of it. She took her house key from her pocket and used it like a dull knife to tear open her wrist. She gritted her teeth against the pain and kept sawing until her blood flowed enough to run and drip. She held her hand inside the hollow until her blood had fallen on the white stone and the soft wood around it.

Before she could withdraw her hand, she felt what was almost a sigh, a ripple of satisfaction that blew over her like a breeze and left her with a sense of the power she had sought. She shivered, suddenly cold. She had what she'd come for, but the thing that gave it had a part of her as well.

***

Tara turned up the volume on the television when her mother came into the house lugging a bag of groceries.

"Get the rest, Tara," she said as she went into the kitchen.

Tara didn't move. Even over the clamor of the sitcom rerun, she could hear the clatter of her mother putting away the groceries and taking out pans so she could start dinner. After a few minutes she appeared in the doorway, a can of corn in her hand.

"I said get the rest of the bags," she said to Tara, raising her voice to be heard.

"I don't want to," Tara said, willing her away, not taking her eyes off the screen.

Her mother strode to the television and turned it off.

"Go get the bags," she said again. "You don't get to opt out."

Tara looked up into her mother's face and called up what she carried.

"I said I don't want to."

Her mother didn't blink this time. She reached out and slapped Tara across the face.

"I've had about enough of your crappy attitude," she said. "I don't know what's the matter with you lately, but this is a family, and you need to help."

Tara jumped to her feet, her hands balled into fists. Her mother's eyes widened.

"Don't you dare," she said. Her mother spotted the bandage wrapped around Tara's wrist, and she reached for her daughter's arm. Tara jerked away.

"What did you do?" her mother asked, anger and fear in her voice. "Tara? What did you do to yourself?"

Tara stood for a moment, caught between what she could do and what she should.

"Leave me alone!" she yelled in her mother's face, her hesitance overwhelmed by the incoherent rage rising up to fill her. For a moment she was lightheaded, and the other force moved her body.

She *pushed.* The power felt like a spasm wringing her strength from her.

Her mother stumbled, then regained her balance. She looked at Tara, her eyes glassy and half-closed. Then she went back out to unload the car herself.

Tara didn't wait for her mother to come back in. She went up to her room and locked the door behind her. Her stomach hurt, and her hands shook as she pulled back the covers and climbed into bed. She would not go back down for dinner. Not tonight.

***

Tara was unsteady when she got up. What had coursed through her left her drained and weak. *That's what it cost,* she thought. But she had gotten what she wanted.

She made her way downstairs, hoping she looked more normal than she felt.

Her mother lay in a heap on the kitchen floor, her face dark with pooled blood, her skin cool and waxy in the morning sun. Tara clapped her hands over her mouth to stifle a scream, then fell to her knees beside her mother's body and shook her shoulder. She already knew it was useless. She tried to summon the wild power she had used to do this, but it was gone. It had done what she wanted, and more. It had done what *it* wanted.

Upstairs, she heard Meggy get out of bed and head into the bathroom.

She couldn't let her sister see this. There was no way to explain it. She had to do something, find some way to fix it. She pinched the skin of her arms hard and forced herself not to think about what she had done to her mother. She couldn't panic now.

When she thought she had a grip on herself, she ran upstairs and knocked at the bathroom door.

"Meggy!" she said against the panels, working to keep her voice even. "Hurry up. I need to show you something."

Meggy pulled the door open.

"What?" she asked.

"The place in the woods where I go. I can show you now if you get dressed. But be quiet. Mom's still sleeping. And she can't know."

***

"I miss the world how it was," Meggy said as they walked down the wooded slope.

"What does that even mean?" Tara asked her sister.

Meggy shrugged and let herself lag behind until Tara stopped and turned to her.

"Come on," she said. "It's just a little bit farther."

Meggy stood still.

"I don't want to go anymore. I want to go home."

Tara struggled to stay calm.

"We can't do that," she said. "We need to go to the place I told you about."

"I want to go home," Meggy said. "I don't want to lie to Mom."

"It's too late," Tara said, fighting the urge to vomit. She grabbed Meggy's shirt and pulled her stumbling along. Meggy started to yell but Tara slapped her until she cried instead.

At the edge of the clearing around the stump, Tara saw a rounded stone that looked as if it had been shaped to fit her hand. She pulled Meggy to the ground and wrapped her fingers around the stone. It was cold against her skin, muddy and rougher than she expected.

She cleared her mind, focusing only on what she wanted this time, and without letting herself form another thought brought the stone down three times onto Meggy's head.

The crack of her skull breaking was like a dull shot in the still space.

Meggy twisted and sighed, still trying to speak. Her eyes rolled in their sockets. Tara didn't think she could see anything.

Hysteria fluttered in Tara's chest, and she bit back a harsh laugh that rose in her throat. She had to finish this.

She smashed Meggy's broken head with the stone until she stopped moving, or speaking, or trying to see.

Tara caught her breath before dragging Meggy's body to the base of the stump. She was cold in the pit of her stomach, numbed even as the rising sun warmed her skin. She wanted to run screaming from this place, knowing what she did. But it was too late for that.

She waited.

The thing turned in its grave among the rocks and roots, deep beneath the shallow memories of the creatures above it. Tara felt it, felt its stirrings and its urges. They were uncomfortable, like a nettle's sting, a lingering pain. What this thing offered, and wanted, did not fit inside her human skin. She shuddered, and stayed. It moved through her, using her senses to touch the world. It felt like nothing she could describe. She scratched at herself, scarcely able to bear it. And then it was gone.

Meggy's hair spread in blood-soaked ropes from the pulpy mess of her skull, tangling with the slithering roots that struggled up from the soil to reach her.

Tara stepped back, afraid the roots would reach for her as well. She leaned carefully forward and placed the bloody stone she still held into the hollow stump. There was a thrumming in the ground now, like a cat's purr. It pushed its way through the soles of her feet, climbing the frame of her muscles and bones, running along her nerves like a current.

It was power. It was an infinite, inexhaustible strength.

It had to be enough.

She stepped over Meggy's body, panting with fear and exultation. She cried now. She could feel the power's potential in the air like a storm about to break. But there was no release.

The pressure was maddening.

"Give me," she demanded, her voice rising to a shout. "I gave to you, now give to me."

For a moment there was only silence, as if the forces she would use were gathering themselves.

What took shape to answer her was an unsettled thing, green and unruly and as new and as ancient as the spring. It rose from the broken stump, sprung from it like a sapling. The roots left Meggy and coiled around it, giving it a physical form. It tasted the blood Tara had spilled for it and wanted more. It was growing, and hungry.

Tara stumbled backward, tripping over masses of coiling roots that moved toward the newborn thing. She had imagined it would look like the green man she had read about, a wild god, something with horns laced in vines and a human face. Not this.

She realized with bleak clarity that sometimes gods are forgotten for a reason. What they give is beyond what a human can use. What they need is beyond what a human can provide. They don't need human attention. They can't remember it.

What she had called up had no need for her at all. But it would still use her.

The thing surged free of the broken tree and reached for her. The arms it embraced her in were stone, and root, and leaf mold, scattered bones and fur and droppings from a thousand generations. They tightened around her like a cleft closing in a rock and buried her beneath the hollow stump with everything else that had gone before. She felt the power of it overfilling her, out of her control. She tried to scream but the breath was crushed from her chest before it could find her voice. All that emerged was a gasp before there was nothing else of her.

And then the woods were quiet again.

***

In the house, warmed by the morning sun streaming in through the kitchen windows, Tara's mother twitched, and stirred, and stood. Her face was mottled with blood. Her skin was as hard as wax.

The sacrifice had almost been enough.

Cut in Marble

I.
ARACHNE AT HER web,
With blithe indifference to her gods—
The hands that made her hands so skilled,
The minds that dreamed her.
She will learn too late
Or never learn
What debt she owes,
And with what blood she must repay it.

II.

I have been everything, incarnate,
Possible and protean,
Promethean, unbounded,
Brought to bay
By other gods.
I have dared excel amidst the mud,
And giving into mortal hands
Have created my own thousand faces.

Pasiphaë

The sun himself my father, you would slander me
that I lay with the ocean's bulls, not even his stallions,
my son a monster by his sire.

You cannot even claim him,
cannot countenance that such a beast is yours.

Instead you give me sin to hide your greed,
that you would keep what you should sacrifice,
cast the weight of your rare insult onto me
since women cannot rule their lust.
Not like you men, with your young gods.
Ask your mother of that.
She gave us monsters of her own.

All the same he is called for you, his father.
History will remember that, if nothing else of us.

As Below, So Above

SHE WILL ALWAYS be just behind me, her hand on my shoulder, her mouth against my ear.

I kept my part of the bargain. I did not look behind me. I did not turn to see if the silence at my back would be my future or my end.

But the gods made Eurydice both.

I thought they loved me, bright Apollo, great Zeus, the rest of them. But in the end, my pain was an amusement for them, to make me dance to their music as they had danced to mine.

***

Eurydice was so beautiful, so right for a wife. They said virgin Artemis favored her family.

I played my lyre for her, as I had for so many before. I beguiled her, as I had so many before. She had no will but to say yes to me, though her eyes betrayed how uncertain she was. She did not love me, but I loved her so. Love could come after.

***

One day soon after our marriage, Eurydice came in from a walk in the woods, flushed and faint. Her women said she had cried out that the wild ones danced among the trees, and as she tried to go to them a fever took her. They brought her home, although she struggled against them.

Despite my pleas, the gods who claimed to love me ignored our suffering.

My Eurydice could not be calmed. She thrashed in her bed, burning and chilled, tormented by pain. After three days the fever broke, and she looked at me with eyes glossed by confusion.

"You are back with us, my love," I whispered, and set to playing to celebrate her recovery.

But she turned away from me, her eyes frightened and her mouth twisted in distaste at my presence.

I thought she was still weak and disoriented by her fever.

I played for her, my song begging her to turn and twine her white arms around me. She should have turned, drawn by the music. But she did not. I called her name, but she did not turn for that either. I gripped her pale shoulder and pulled her to face me. Her eyes were round with surprise.

"Eurydice, my wife," I said, and her mouth opened like a black cave and she howled. She shook her head back and forth as if to shake off a swarm of bees.

"No, no, no!" she cried, her voice flat and garbled.

I sang out her name again, strummed the strings of the lyre, but she grew more agitated, more wild. It struck me suddenly that she could not hear me to be calmed. The fever had stolen her hearing. I could no longer entangle her heart.

***

I gave orders that she be watched through the night as I made my sacrifices to bright Apollo, to beg him to heal her and give her back to me.

But her women feared her bleatings and her wild eyes, and did not try to stop her when she fled my house for the dark of the forest. Her women sat with stony faces when I returned, saying only that she was gone where she would, and it was not for them to bar her way.

After I had them beaten, I called my servants to me, and with the dawn we braved the rustling, shadowed forest to seek my mad Eurydice.

We found her soon enough.

She lay at the base of an ancient oak, her cold body barely draped in her torn robe. Her face was as dark as a Gorgon's, her hair tangled with twigs, her white eyes staring at nothing. Her ankle bore the twin scars of a serpent's bite.

I do not remember the journey home. My servants say they carried my dead Eurydice between them, and I walked behind them like a ghost.

***

Eurydice was buried.

I did not see it. I hid in my rooms.

I did not eat, and only slept when exhaustion forced it on me. I played dark songs upon my lyre and prayed to all my gods. I wept, and I bargained, and I sang to sway their divine attentions.

Eventually bright Apollo sent me a sign, a direction to take. I could travel to the underworld and win back my beloved wife. I could, if I dared.

I prepared myself with sweet oils and a crown of flowers, as I had for my wedding. I bade my men open the tomb that held Eurydice. I made new sacrifices to Apollo, to Zeus, to Hades. And then I walked through the mouth of the tomb and into the underworld.

I was alone for the longest time, or only a moment. Time is nothing in the Kingdom of the Dead. I played and sang as I travelled, the only living creature in all the underworld.

Suddenly, a sharp whisper cut through my song and silenced me. Before me, where there had only been a grey fog, stood a pair of thrones carved from black stone. Upon one sat a misty, shrouded, silent figure with the shape of a man. On the other sat a pale woman whose fingers gripped the stone beneath her.

"Mortal," she said in the same sharp whisper. "We have heard your pleas. Your song is persuasive. I know something of the bonds of marriage."

The silent figure shifted beside his queen.

"Eurydice is willing to be with you again. We will allow her to leave these halls."

I cried out in joy, and cast about to see my beloved wife.

"Quiet here," the pale queen warned me. "She may leave only if you trust that she follows you, and you do not look back to see her until you stand once more in the sun."

"Yes!" I swore. "I will not look for her if it means I may have her!"

The queen smiled, a terrible thing.

"Then go," she said. "And know that after this, we shall never help you again."

And I was alone, in a vast and echoing place. Except I was not alone. At my shoulder, a shadow. Eurydice.

"My love," I breathed. "I have come to bring you home."

At my ear, a hissing breath.

"I will follow you always."

How my heart lifted, how my songs rang out in the dim grey mist!

I walked, and at intervals called over my shoulder to my beloved wife.

And she answered, always.

In what could have been a hundred years or only an hour, I saw the mouth of the tomb open before me, and I stepped over its threshold into the yellow light of day. I walked a few steps more, to give Eurydice room to leave her grave.

The men who had opened the tomb stood as if only moments had passed. They looked at me until one asked me if I had gone in yet.

"But I am back already," I said. "Can you not see my Eurydice behind me?"

The man looked at his fellows and at the space where I knew my wife stood.

"No," he said. "It is as if you had yet to go."

At that I angrily told the men to close the tomb and be gone.

I turned to look my beloved in the face, but she was not there. Only the sting of her breath at my ear.

"I will follow you always."

I turned again, and again, but could not catch even a glimpse of her bright eyes, of her brown hair.

All I could get of her was her soft, hissing voice, reminding me.

Of a sudden I knew that it was no promise I wanted. I grew frightened then, and wild with what I had done.

I ran through the town to my home, ran into my chamber, and threw myself upon my bed. My lyre broke beneath me, but I could not care. Over my shoulder Eurydice whispered my name, the weight of her anger upon it.

Bright Apollo had hinted at what could be possible, that what I wished might be true.

From his hints I have made my own hell, and the gods smiled as I did it.

I knew then what I had won.

I found a dagger in my cabinet and drove it into my heart. I felt my body die, for the briefest moment, before my heart beat again. I called my servants and demanded they bring me arsenic and wine. I drank it down, and heaved and spasmed, died and lived despite it.

All the time, she stayed by me. Always.

Pale Persephone said they would not help me again. I must always survive.

And now Eurydice hovers, hissing her devotion, with the serpent that killed her still wound around her poisoned heart.

SEALS

SHE WAS OLDER than he had first thought when he noticed her rummaging around on the rocks, down near the water line. Her motion drew his eyes. It was only when she clambered up toward where he stood, as she turned her face up and smiled squinting into the sun to see him, that he noticed the fine mist of age on her face. She was plain, not striking, and further on than forty. But she climbed the tumbled boulders smoothly, as sure of her footing as a young animal.

He stepped back as she reached the clifftop, giving her room. He looked out past her shoulder at the sea behind her, at the waves breaking against broken stone. Gulls wheeled through the sky, far out over the water.

She dusted her hands against her flanks before extending one to him.

"Seems we're the only ones out today. Hi. Cynthia."

"Cynthia, hi. I'm Peter," he answered, taking her proffered hand. Her grip was strong and he returned it in kind. She grinned at him, long teeth in a sharp smile.

"Late in the season for vacationing," she said. He could not place her accent. It wasn't local.

"Yes," Peter said. "I couldn't get away from work before now. Beautiful country though, even this late."

She nodded, still smiling, with no reply.

"It's better now, actually. Fewer people around. I'm staying on the point, at the Driftwood," he added.

"Nice place. Nice people."

Peter had the feeling the conversation was done. She still kept her friendly expression, still kept her mouth in its curve, but something had come into her eyes that let him think he might be overstaying his welcome. She perched at the edge of the cliff where she had first climbed up, territorial. He brushed away the idea, but it hovered.

"Yes," he said, taking his chance to retreat from the conversation. "Cynthia, I'm sure I'll see you again. I just got in this afternoon and still haven't unpacked."

"Of course," she replied. "Enjoy yourself."

He stepped back toward the rough path to the road, dismissed. Cynthia passed him, slipping around him at the mouth of the path. She waved loosely over her shoulder as she negotiated the trail through the low scrub of blueberry, juniper, and wild roses, watching her feet as she went. Peter waited until she was around the first curve before he turned back to the rocks.

He climbed down to the first wide ledge, cautious in street shoes, and peered down the route he had seen Cynthia take. There, ten yards down and above the level of the low tide, was a dead seal, intact but for the blood staining the fur around its empty eyes.

***

The lodging Peter decided on was a collection of old clapboard houses and prefabricated cottages clustered on a curve of high rocks at the edge of the sea, a draw for city dwellers to come to watch the wild Atlantic. Peter felt vaguely out of place. He was obviously less wealthy than the other guests. He was glad he had splurged on a housekeeping cabin instead of staying in the main house, where he would have to tolerate the common areas or hide in his room. It was his first real vacation in years, an indulgence and reward for being gainfully employed in his field for the first time since finishing graduate school. He had chosen this place almost by accident, heading north on the flip of a coin and following the coastline the entire way. Maine's Calendar Islands intrigued him, and here he was, on the southernmost spit of land in Casco Bay. The otherness in the place filled him, the raw age of the rocks beneath his feet, the alien weight of the ocean. This, more than anywhere he had ever been, reminded him how old the world was, and how tenuous a hold men had on it. There was no mercy in the great ocean crashing on the rocks, and no cruelty. It was, and nothing more.

His cabin fronted a bare strip of sand between rocky arms. A wild rose grew beside the steps to the painted wooden porch, with deep pink flowers still flagrantly blooming in late October. Peter leaned over to breathe in the lingering scent of summer.

The cabin, once a single large room, had been divided by walls that did not reach the beamed ceiling. The interior was all pine—real wood instead of paneling, golden and glossy with varnish. He dropped his duffel bag on one of the twin beds in the rear bedroom. He wouldn't use those beds. The front room had seaward-facing windows, a dining table, and a futon. He left the door wide open behind him and pushed up the windows to let in the sharp breeze. Bright sun reached to the back of the cabin. Peter sat down on the futon where he could look out the door and let himself simply be.

***

The inn's main building stood on cliffs made by granite slabs shearing off into the sea. It had a covered patio where guests could enjoy the view. Peter took nearly solitary advantage of it. A number of people were staying in the main house, but Peter saw them only in passing. They appeared to be mostly well-heeled couples wearing ensembles ill-suited to the rocky island, which mattered very little since they also seemed uninterested in the outdoors. They travelled from their cars to the inn and back again in rotation, enjoying the salt air only as they moved through it to somewhere else. As he sat on the patio with his lunch, Peter wondered idly why they had even come. From this vantage, the ocean was all there was to see. This was the last island jutting into the bay. Beyond it was only the long unfurling of the Atlantic.

A thin dirt path snaked along the side of the patio, skirting the shallow rock face. Peter was curious but not surprised when Cynthia appeared around the corner of the inn and headed down the path. She had not seen him there in the cool shadows, and she turned with a strange look on her face when he hailed her.

"It's a small island," she said, waving her hand at the air. "I usually do this from the water, but I left the kayak home today."

She leaned against the patio railing and tilted back the broad-brimmed sun hat she wore. "Care to come along?" Bored, Peter stretched and climbed over the railing to join her.

The path was broken where it switched back on itself along the steep cliff. Cynthia led the way, and Peter again let his eyes follow her movements. She was compelling. Her clothes were stained, as if they had been wet and dried and worn again without washing. He was glad of his hiking boots, for despite Cynthia's ease the trail was tricky to navigate. At the base she led him west around and over outcroppings, and finally up again to an isolated ledge away from the trail. Peter could see the waterline below them, see where Cynthia's route would be submerged when the tide rose. She drew his attention back to the rock where they stood. "Look," she said, pointing to a hollow formed over centuries by wind and scouring sand. Cradled in the rock were a doglike skull and a handful of worn bones the color of old ivory. The stub of a thick white candle stood pasted to the rock with wax.

"I collect them," she said, tapping the dome of the skull. Peter realized these were seal bones. He ignored the candle's insinuation of ritual.

She pulled a clicking handful of teeth from her pocket, sharp yellow things from a hunter's jaw. She laid them gently beside the weathered skull and the scattered spill of vertebrae. "Still want to get a whole skin," she said, a laugh in her voice. Peter cringed. She caught his reaction, a hunter herself.

"You don't want to see this," she said, her words flat, her eyes hooded by the shadow of her hat brim.

"Why do you keep them here? Why don't you just take them home?" Peter said. He felt her closing against him, returning him to a stranger.

"I'm sorry," he said, talking past his disquiet. "I don't understand what you want with them."

She squeezed past him on the ledge, as balanced as a dancer. "I'll take you back," she said. Any welcome she had offered had been rescinded.

Peter followed her in silence, chastened like a schoolboy.

***

He did not see Cynthia for several days, but he could not rid himself of the feeling that she was nearby, avoiding him. Curious, he sought out the owner of the inn in his office and asked if he knew her.

"I've seen her around," the man said after considering Peter's description. "Not lately though. She's never come in."

"Do you know where she lives?" Peter said.

"Couldn't say," he said. The man turned back to his ledger. "Far as I know, she doesn't bother with anybody."

Peter let it go. Cynthia could be his mystery. He biked to the souvenir shop at the far tip of the island, and to the bay where the lobster boats anchored. He bought expensive provisions at the tiny general store rather than driving to the mainland, and found a farm stand that sold raw milk and local vegetables. He fished the cove for mackerel and pollock. The days were clear and temperate, with the chill of autumn held off by the expansive, warm Atlantic. He relaxed in the solitude.

***

A storm rolled in on the night of the full moon. At high tide, Peter stood on the cabin's porch to watch how high the waves clawed up the narrow beach. He wondered if they would reach him. Lightning shattered in the sky, cast jagged light across the churning water. Gusts of wind drove the rain sideways through the air. Peter shut the door against the wind and went back to the warm safety of the futon. He listened to the crash and rumble of the storm as he read himself to sleep.

He awoke to pounding on the heavy wooden door. Startled and groggy, Peter pulled the blankets with him as he stumbled up to answer it. In the storm, electrified as if a part of it, was Cynthia.

"Let me in," she said, and he did.

She was dripping, her long hair as tangled as the waves. Peter stepped away from her, awake now.

"The kayak's in the cove," she said. "Damn thing filled up. It's on the bottom now. Hope it's still there when the storm breaks, but I'm not counting on it."

"You were out there in this?"

Cynthia grinned, mirthless. "Can I have a towel?"

Peter grabbed a dishtowel from the kitchen and tossed it to her over the half-wall that separated the kitchen from the front room. Then he grabbed himself a beer from the refrigerator. He stayed in the kitchen. The clock read ten thirty. Cynthia's presence ate away at what peace he had found. She made him uncomfortable in his own skin, like an infection, an itch. He drank his beer in long gulps, but he could not stop glancing toward her. He watched her rubbing her hair dry with the small cloth. He went to the back bedroom for a larger towel and dry clothing.

"Here," he said, handing her the bundle. She took it from him, avoiding his hands. For a moment it was so quiet in the cabin that he could hear the water drip from her clothes to the floor. Then a gust rattled the windows with gunfire rain.

"Thank you," she said solemnly. She began to pull her soaked top off, and Peter turned away.

"This is supposed to blow through by dawn," he said, busying himself in the kitchen again. He realized it was an invitation. He kept his eyes down but still caught glimpses of Cynthia drying off and changing. He pulled a pot of stew from the refrigerator. "Are you hungry?"

"No," she said, looking over the dividing wall at him, small inside his clothes. "But I'll take tea if you have it."

He did. He put on a kettle of water to heat, got out a mug, the tea, the sugar, and milk. "Why were you out there?"

"You don't really want to know," she said, too familiar.

"You're lucky you weren't killed."

"Yes. I am," she said. She went to the front window and pulled the curtain aside. Outside, the storm lashed the sky. Wind cried around the tight cabin with the voice of a lost child. Peter brought their drinks to the table. At last she turned away from the window and joined him. "Seals don't care if it's storming. They have to hunt, they have to eat," she said.

Smirking with anticipation, she sipped at her too-hot tea.

"Have you ever seen one come through?" she said.

"Seen what?" he said.

"A seal. The fish disappear. They look at you with those big, wet eyes like they're puppies or something, but all they are are scavengers and predators. Men have to make a living."

She mimed shooting a pistol at Peter to make her point. He looked at her without expression, hoping his lack of response would discourage her.

"The seals rob the traps. It's like a free lunch for them. The bait's not good enough, they take the shedders too, the lobsters with new shells, easy eating. So the lobstermen kill them when they can. The seals think they're high on the food chain. But they're not the highest."

Peter drained his beer and set the bottle down carefully on the table.

"You know a lot about them."

"I have to," she said.

Peter left her words alone.

Cynthia leaned back in her chair, her hands wrapped around the hot mug.

"Where are you staying?" he asked.

"Around."

"It's too nasty out there for you to go out again," Peter said after a moment. "You can have the bedroom and go in the morning."

Cynthia looked at him steadily. Her eyes, he noticed, were grey.

"I don't mean to make you uncomfortable, Peter. I appreciate your hospitality. I'll be going to bed now, and get out of your way."

With that she retired to the back of the cabin. He heard her hanging up her sopping clothes in the tiny bathroom, and he heard the slip of the sheets being pulled back. Then nothing. As he settled himself into the warm nest of the futon, he realized there was no sense of another living thing in the cabin. The rise and fall of the storm had become monotony, and it took Peter a long time of staring into the darkness before he fell back to sleep.

***

She was gone when he awoke. He had half-expected it. It was still raining fitfully, but the wind had died and the sky was a patchy blue where the clouds broke apart. Peter wandered into the bedroom. The sheets and blanket were folded back on one of the beds but it did not look as though anyone had slept there. A small puddle remained on the bathroom floor, and the towel she had used hung smoothly over the side of the shower stall.

When the tide turned and the remnants of the storm dissolved into a clear day, Peter walked out to his beach. A few yards out he could see the bright yellow hull of Cynthia's kayak breaking through the surface of the water. He went back to the cabin for his tall rubber boots, then waded carefully into the shallow water. The rocks underfoot were slippery with algae, and clumps of seaweed torn loose by the storm wrapped around his ankles as he went. Peter balanced himself carefully as he gripped the edge of the kayak's cockpit and dragged it toward the beach. Once he had it almost out of the water, he tipped it up to drain it. Something rattled inside the hull, and he stiffened at the sound but did not look for its source. He got the kayak up on the beach and left it to dry out in the sun.

Peter stretched his back and looked out over the length of the cove at the empty ocean beyond it. His eyes followed the curving rocks that swept back to his beach. A grey shape lay against them in the shallow water there, abandoned by the sea. He had not noticed it while he was busy with the kayak. He waded out to it and looked down on the smooth-furred body rolled gently by the waves. Sometimes the lapping motion would turn it just so, and it would look back at him from its empty sockets. He leaned closer to the seal's corpse with grim interest. It still had its teeth.

***

Cynthia turned up again two days later to return his clothes. They were dry and neatly folded, smelling of salt and her body. Peter took them from her but did not invite her in.

"Your kayak is over there," he said, pointing with his chin.

"I saw it. Thank you," she answered, holding his eyes with hers. "It's alright then?"

"I didn't see any damage. You were an idiot to be out in that. You shouldn't be here now after that risk."

Cynthia smiled, cold. "Of course. You're right."

Peter looked past her to the glittering sea. This was not the vacation he had envisioned when he arrived. He stood there in awkward audience to her, at a loss for conversation. She waited before him, neutral should he respond.

A young couple emerged from the inn, the wife carrying a small boy like an accessory, and climbed into a sleek sedan. Peter watched them go, and Cynthia turned to see what had his attention. When she faced him again her mouth was pursed with caustic humor. "Not quite our type, are they?" she said.

"I don't get you," Peter said.

She looked into his face, looked away. Her own face was unreadable. "No."

He took a step backward, away from her. In the clean morning sun, she seemed too strange a companion, not someone Peter would or should associate with. But she had her own tidal pull.

Cynthia shifted her weight to one leg, her hips canted in an adolescent attitude. She gestured to the kayak.

"I'm going around the point. Follow me."

Peter pressed the clothes he held against his belly.

"There's only the one kayak."

"Follow me on the cliffs. You can circle most of the island along them."

Peter nodded, a thrill of nerves rising in his chest. She drew him, and he wished to be drawn.

Peter went into the cabin while she prepared herself, calmer away from her. He watched her through the open window. She had scrounged up a new paddle somewhere, and a tattered orange fabric life vest that would not meet even decade-old standards. She dragged the kayak to the edge of the water, letting the sandy gravel support it as she climbed in. When she shoved off into the cove, floating free, he came back out and walked up alongside the inn. She saw him and pointed out her trajectory with the paddle blade, like a pool player calling her shot. Peter waved and followed her as she cleared the confines of the cove and struck the unsheltered sea.

Passing before the inn, Peter followed the sketch of path and kept an eye on Cynthia for his bearings. She traced the line of the cliffs from a distance, wary of the suck of the waves. Peter took his time on the rough ground. His course led through private properties and he had to find passage up and down the face of the rocks, braced always to hear the rapid bark of a guard dog or the yell of a defending homeowner. Nothing came, this late in the season. The houses were closed up except for their caretakers. The inn was far behind him. Between the sea and the empty houses, he was alone. His skin prickled with it.

He grew heated in the sun. Sweat soaked his hair beneath his hat despite a clean breeze off the water. He paused in the shadow of a shallow overhang, wiping his face and casting about for Cynthia. He had lost track of her for a moment, outpaced her.

The distance between them could not be great. He had only just missed her. He strained against the glare of the sun on the water for a flash of the yellow hull. The sea gave him nothing. He thought he heard a thin cry, but it did not repeat. It might have been a gull. He might have imagined it. He waited, then cupped his hands around his mouth and bellowed her name over the crash of the tide. He listened for any response. She could not be gone so quickly. He scanned the roiled plane of the sea for anything that might point to her. Through the flicker of sunlight, he saw long, dark shapes in the water, scattered among the waves and moving fast across them. A sleek head broke the surface and slipped under again, then another, another, like a string of beads, seals in sequence drawing breath.

Peter stepped to the brink of the trail where the ledge dropped off into air to be closer to the seals as they swam. He had never seen seals in the wild before. They reminded him of a wolfpack. The last in line rolled onto its back and looked up at him. Then it dove and disappeared after the rest.

Below him, a wave boomed against the rocks hard enough to throw spray up against his legs. He glanced down and saw the yellow kayak rolling on the rocks, trapped by the incessant incoming surf. He stared at it, blank. It tumbled back and away like a metronome, and echoed hollowly as each wave hit it. He could only watch it, thinking that maybe Cynthia would pop out from among the rocks and hail him. At last, the empty kayak caught the curl of a wave and filled, slipping down, becoming a fading blur under the unquiet water. He had not realized how deep the sea was here, how far down the rocks went into the belly of the water. He still cast about for Cynthia, calling for her to answer.

At a crease in the wet rocks, he thought he saw the pale bend of an arm. The water surged over it, and he thought he could see a bloated hand dangle and flop. He looked for a way to get to it, and picked his way down the cliff face until he hung just above it. The waves rolled in and lifted a soft white body caught in the crevice. Her swollen face floated up with mouth agape and eyes picked out. He closed his eyes tightly and held to the rocks. What he had seen had been in the water for days. In his darkness Peter told himself that it might be a drowned bird, or a fish, or torn seaweed. He needed the uncertainty. When he opened his eyes, he looked only up and climbed back to the path.

He waited then, vacant. Time passed slowly as he stood, the light moving down the sky. The ocean heaved and swelled, unreadable, without memory. Gulls skirled above him against bright blue and clouds. He squinted up at them, watching for a long while the glide of their wings on the air before he turned away. With his hands in his pockets, he faced into the wind and walked away from the cliff edge up to the road. She would not be coming.

THE WIND, THE SAND

SCALES SLIDE ACROSS each other with a sound like sand blowing over stone.

My sister cries, somewhere above me, somewhere higher than I can see.

My eyes feel as if sand blows across them. My vision is blurred.

I am not breathing.

I rise and wipe the grit from my face, my clouded eyes, my wet mouth. I shake the dust of the street from my hair and my skirts. I walk.

Above me, wind cuts across the sky with a sound like leathery wings beating. I open my mouth, hoping that some of the wind will fill me, that some of the beating rhythm will restore me.

It does not.

My sister's crying becomes a distant whimper, all around me in the dusty air.

I walk away from it, down the empty, narrow street, past the tall city walls, into the wide, empty desert. I wipe the blowing sand away from my eyes, and I can see again.

The city is smaller than it felt from inside its walls, the desert far, far more vast. In the sky, beside the pale rind of the moon, a tiny figure dips and glides. Even at this distance I can hear its scales click against each other as it turns.

The wind fills my open mouth with sand and dust. It fills my throat, trickles down into my lungs, my guts. But I am not breathing. All its weight can do is anchor me here.

I walk now, more slowly. I do not tire. I do not thirst, even as the wide desert teases the last moisture from my mouth, from my eyes. Even dry as dust, I move steadily forward. The wind follows me now.

Above me in the pale sky I see the long, twining figure cut circles in the air, sweeping closer, sweeping down. It is a beast, a serpent. It cuts the air with long wings that make the sound of a whip crack as they beat. Over its narrow head like a corona hangs a sharp slice of silver, an echo of the moon.

Scales scrape against my hands as I draw the serpent down, its wings beating slowly against the heated air, stirring clouds of dust that dissipate above us. It lands beside me. Its long neck lifts from the sand, its long jaws open in a hiss that is not breath.

It does not breathe either.

Cradled between its wings is a figure as dry and breathless as I am, its hand on the serpent's neck, its head turning this way and that, searching. It cannot find me, though, as it casts about. It has no eyes. It cannot see.

I let the wind and dust wheeze out of my mouth, and its blind face turns to me as a flower seeks the sun. I step forward and put my hand over its hand on the serpent's neck, and help it climb down onto the soft and moving sand. I hold its shoulders so that it faces me, study its blind face, peer into the caverns of its lost eyes.

It sags, dust drifting from its dry mouth, sifting off its tight dry skin. It is not who it used to be. It is not who I remember, who I once mourned. I ease it down onto the sand. The wind passes over us, blowing sand across its still face, filling its empty eye sockets and open mouth, erasing its details beneath the swallowing dust.

I pull the long scythe free of its dry hand. I feel the weight of it. I study the dull gleam. Already my eyes are dimmer than they were before I took the blade.

The serpent twines its way to me and I mount it, scales catching and tearing my dusty skirts. Its body is cool beneath me as it lifts us into the sky. My hand is on its neck. My hand is on the scythe's handle. We soar among the clouds of dust, among the blowing scrape of sand.

Already my eyes are polished and worn by the sand that flies in them.

I steer the serpent by the pressure of my hand, back to the city, over its high walls. While I still have sight, I must take my turn, cull the masses, reap the harvest.

I cannot seek my home until my eyes are worn away and I am blind.

Just as my mother before me.

Far below, I can still hear my sister's cries.

I hope she will have stopped her grieving by the time these scaled wings bring me to her again.

III.
WHAT COMES AFTER

THE FIRE THIS TIME

SHE SQUATS ON the ridge of the hill, her elbows on her knees, her skinny butt pressed against her ankles, watching the fires. Occasionally she reaches over to scratch the head of the rangy dog lazing beside her, its tongue lolling out and its eyes alert. The scratching makes a thick sound; both the dog and her hands are very dirty. The fires ebb and flow like tides, washing across the rolling land, receding again, leaving scattered yellow sparks in their wake. She lets herself fall into a lull, watching without focusing. Time is measured in the motion of the flames. Faint heat carries on the wind.

She has no idea what could still be burning down there. It is easier not to think about it.

The dog groans happily and pushes its nose against her leg. She keeps scratching, absent-minded. They are a pair in this empty world. The dog found her, one day before things got too bad, before the city had become nothing but ash and embers with nothing left to salvage. She was gathering what she could still use of all the abandoned things. The dog had been left behind, or had refused to go when its owners left. It came trotting out from the crisp remains of a landscaped yard and fell into step beside her as she walked through the neat, vacated neighborhood. She did not slow down, and the dog nudged at her fingers without breaking pace. She rubbed its ears, and their association began.

She is already regretting the day she and the dog would no longer be friends, when each would have to decide the other was food. She tries not to think that far ahead. They are alright for now; the situation is grim but not yet hopeless, or it is hopeless but she does not know it yet.

**

She wasn't paying attention when the fires began, or even much while they were happening. Her boyfriend would watch the news during dinner, avid and silent, and she would sit beside him and let it all wash past her. He tried to make her notice it, paraphrasing events as if speaking to a small child: "The brushfires are bad this summer. Every time you turn on the news they're threatening another development, people are being evacuated left and right." The disasters and mayhem were too much to absorb, so she simply did not. Climate change, sunspots, divine retribution—she had no idea. Her thoughts had always been elsewhere. It was almost like motion at the periphery of her vision; she knew something had shifted, but turned too late to see what it had been.

It never seemed to end, the news and his commentary. It was a bad summer in general. The heat was oppressive, the fires turned the coast into a wall of smoke, and she was on another downward spiral. He must have recognized it, she thought now. The constant pressure to make her follow the news must have been his attempt to keep her from disappearing again. After three years together, six assorted shrinks, and one involuntary hospitalization, he must have been trying to save her. He loved her, after all. She knew that. She just did not have the strength to listen. And then things got very quiet. He stopped talking to her one day, and eventually she noticed his silence. She was left to herself behind her dead-eyed stare.

She could not remember what had happened to him. One day she dully realized he wasn't there anymore. She thought it was not too long after the real trouble started that he left. She wasn't sure if it was because they were already drifting away from each other and he was just too tired of trying, or if it were a direct result of the changes in the wider world. She hoped distantly that it was because of the fires. With effort she dragged one memory from her unsullied mind, one sharp flash of connection. He had said at some point he was going east to Pennsylvania, to take care of his parents, to get away from *this*. He never defined *this*. He didn't take anything with him, not his books or his razor or his bottles of wine. He had not asked her to come with him. He had not asked if she were going to leave as well. She hadn't heard from him since then.

***

Eventually, bit by bit, it penetrated her soft shell that she was alone. The quiet was a force of its own. Not only had her boyfriend left, but her neighbors, and strangers, and all. She had no idea where they had gone. She had a vague sense that they had moved away, simply got in their cars and driven to someplace else that was not burning down.

Maybe they had all gone east. She was not privy to the message they had received telling them to go. Everyone had gone, no goodbyes, no packing, just suddenly not there. Everything they had left behind had been slowly consumed—the city and suburbs a lacework of glowing embers for weeks before the neatly spaced buildings finally crumpled softly in upon themselves.

She didn't think to call anyone, not friends, not family, to ask them what they were going to do, where they were going to go. She was long out of the habit of speaking to anyone. In her sole attempt to ease the silence, she found that radio had disappeared into a haze of static; perhaps the smoke so weighted the air that no signal could get through. The last time she had bothered to check, there was still the internet. She wasn't sure how long ago she had last logged on—before the evacuations, she thought, but how long before? Whether there was anyone on the other side was still a mystery. She was too incurious to look for news, and left the television turned off. She didn't really want to know.

She stayed in their apartment by herself for a while, sifting through the artifacts of her own belongings as the other inhabitants of the building trickled away. She aimlessly emptied her drawers of all her clothing, unpacked boxes from the depths of the closet that still held her favored childhood dolls. She straightened their dresses, smoothed down their dull hair, unstuck eyes that should close when the doll tipped backward. She lined them all up against the windows, looking out. Watching the world.

The block emptied, and the town. The birds were gone, the squirrels, all the rustling things that had lived there in the ornamental trees. Even the insects had fled, or burned. Water still came from the faucet, but it was a brown trickle, unpleasant to drink. The world was winding down. She and her dolls watched the fires move implacably closer, eating away everything in their way, until the soft fall of ash pattering like forgotten rain woke her to the fact that she was still in their path. Then, with no one to bid goodbye, she left as well. Only the dolls watched her leave. She looked back up at their blank plastic faces, wondering if one of them would wave to her before she headed away.

She headed east as her boyfriend had, away from the drifting flames, into the hills above the city. There were vacation homes up there, scattered places where she might be safe. There did not seem to be any cars left behind, so she went on foot. She did not run. There was no need for headlong panic. She wandered, took her time, found a child's red wagon on her way and loaded it with left-behind food. Few people, it seemed, had locked their doors behind them. The dog found her. She and the dog eventually found the cabin.

The flames lapped around the hills, but her cabin was safe, for now, far above the burn line. She could make her stand in the cabin. It was dated but homey, with wood-framed furniture and printed curtains, mismatched dishes and a minimum of pots and pans. There was a flagpole beside the door, but she couldn't find the flag. The cabin had running water too, by what mechanism or miracle she did not know or wonder, afraid to break the spell. She took it for the sheer blind luck that it was. She and the dog went back and forth to the suburbs several times, filling the wagon with any canned and packaged goods she could find and hauling it back. There was less than she thought there would be; it seemed the food was often dried up within its wrappings, unusable. But it was more than nothing, and filled the empty closet in the cabin with some sense of hope.

After she settled in, she had walked half a day farther out, past the arms of the fire, but there were no more cabins, no more water, only a grey and yellow landscape relentlessly drying up. It was far enough for now, would have to be, until the flames flowed uphill and overtook her. But now she had time.

***

She pulls herself back to the world, drowsy from the patterns the flames make, her eyes sore. The fires are beginning to reach around the hills, closing the circle slowly. The wind has shifted; smoke taints the air. She stands, arches her back hard with her hands bracing her waist. She does not want to consider moving on, not again. Behind the haze that never quite clears, the sky is beginning to deepen toward evening. The dog jumps up, eager to follow her home.

She leaves the door open behind her when she enters, no need to block the light, no need to guard against no one. The dog trots in and out, impatient for dinner. But he must wait. The first thing she does each evening when she returns is a brazen indulgence. Far away from this she knows she should not do it. She turns the taps on the kitchen sink and lets the water run, looking forward to rinsing the rime of smoke and dust from her face.

It has been a long time since she has been completely clean. Since she found the cabin, she has showered only once, afraid to waste what she cannot replace. Each time she returned to the suburbs she tested the faucets in random houses. There was never more than a muddy seep to stain her fingers. The fires have boiled it away.

Tonight the water spits and pops through the faucet, displaced by air in the pipes but still trying to flow. It has done this more often lately, and her heart catches each time until the water pushes through. The interval grows too long. Nothing flows. She turns the taps, knowing at a remove that it is useless but disbelieving. The basin is half-full of cool water. She feels a knot tighten in her throat. She shoves her index finger into the end of the faucet, breaking the thin screen there, feeling for any obstruction. There is none. She briefly imagines dismantling the plumbing, making it work again. The idea slips away.

Without the inexplicable flow of water, everything she has tuned out or does not know is upon her. She cannot fix this. She doesn't know what has happened. It is too late to find out now. The interlude of safety is ended, and the world has come crashing through. This is worse than when her boyfriend left her behind, or when the city emptied around her and she passively, dumbly stayed. That was numbing inertia; this is nothing but helplessness.

The dog can tell something is wrong, and presses its nose into her hand. She is unresponsive, caught. Her fingers move of their own accord, scratching the dog's muzzle and throat. She doesn't want the dog to die. She lets her head drop forward, lets her filthy hair cover her eyes. She doesn't want the stupid dog to die.

Without warning she smacks the dog hard on the nose, yelling at it, her voice grainy with disuse. She claps her hands over its head, driving it out of the cabin with her noise. She chases the dog away, but it comes back when she stops ranting. It wags its tail hopefully, ears pricked forward for any encouragement. The dog comes toward her with its head low, and simpers at her feet. She can't think; the dog will die here without her. It is as foolish as she is. She kicks it hard in the ribs. The dog yelps and runs around the corner of the cabin. She can hear its crackling progress through the desiccated woods. Better the dog hates her. Better it goes away.

She goes back into the cabin and shuts the door, latches it. It feels necessary to bolt the door now. Now there is something to fear out there, and the lock is all the protection she has. The dog will probably come back, thinking this is still its home. She hopes it will not. Things have changed here. She will not open the door for it if it does.

Her shoulders slump as she stands over the sink. She lets her hands drop into the bowl, lets the last of the water ripple over her skin. She looks at her ragged hands beneath the surface of the water. She will not be so lucky again, no matter how far east she goes. If she goes. From a shadowy corner of memory, she recalls fragments of stories she has read, musings on flesh and bone as the characters face their mortality. In fiction there is wisdom and a final grace. Here, there is nothing but dust.

She lets the water out of the basin, watches it flow away in a last tiny whirlpool through the silver ring of the drain. She wipes her hands around the inside of the bowl, gathering up the cool remains of moisture, and smooths them over her face.

Ash drifts down against the windows, hot and soft. If she closes her eyes, she can almost hear it rain.

ꝒREDATION

SHE SAW IT first as a ripple in the night, a deeper shadow against the deep blue sky.

The seven dogs in the yard barked wildly, harsh phlegmy cries that verged on screaming. She rose from her bed, went to the window but did not open it, peered through the thin safety of the glass at the moonlit chaos below her. The dogs churned on their chains and howled.

Then something dark moved across the corner of the yard, and they cowered and whined and fell silent. Fine hairs lifted on her arms and neck, and she craned forward to see through her own reflection. The figure had a human shape, but was no more than that in the spare blue light. She watched it dip over a huddled dog, and the rest of the animals exploded again into frenzy.

She stepped back from the window, away from the revealing moonlight. Her skin was sensitized to the cool air as if it were wet. She was afraid to move.

Eventually the dogs grew quiet, their voices paled to whimpers. She edged closer to the window, slow as frost, until she could see her yard. The shape had gone. The dogs would keep until morning. She climbed back into her bed and pulled the quilts over her face, and lay perfectly still, invisible, until sleep at last took her.

In the clear light of morning, the yard was a tableau. The living dogs were dazed, exhausted, their eyes white with fear. She was glad they were chained. Two dead dogs near the fence lay in dark stains of their wasted blood, reduced to dirty piles. She prodded one with her toe, flipped it over. Broken bones and ripped throat lay open to the sunlight. It was already beginning to rot. No meat gone that she could tell. She contemplated the damage, her hands on her hips. Then she tilted her head back and gazed up into the sky, drawing clean air into her lungs.

She dragged the dogs' corpses to the dump behind the barn and burned them. The flames were almost invisible in the sunlight, but the fire was too hot to stand near. She fed the pyre a steady diet of scrap wood until she was sure nothing that could rise remained.

***

The day was chilly but she drove her truck with the windows down to wash the smell of the fire out of her hair. The roads were empty. They were usually empty. The town had contracted as the plague came through, paring down to the real locals.

She pulled in next to two other pickup trucks in front of the grocery store. It seemed everyone left in town drove pickups now.

The cowbell tied to the door handle announced her with a flat clang. No other customers were in the store. The owner looked out of the back room, an open bag of chips in his hand. She waved him back as she took a cart to fill with supplies. He came out again as she was finishing her shopping.

"Hey, Bob," she said as she approached the counter.

"Hannah. Everything okay out there?"

She unloaded her groceries slowly. "Something came after my dogs last night. Got two of them."

Bob whistled through his teeth. "I know I always say it, but you've got to move closer."

"I know."

He rang up her items and she bagged them up in canvas totes.

"I also need diesel for the generator."

Bob paused in his tallying. "I can only sell you ten gallons for now. Truck didn't make it in yet."

"That won't last me any time at all."

"Best I can do."

Hannah hefted the full totes. "When is it coming?"

"Don't know. It was coming from Philly. There's been no word."

She sighed. "Alright. I'll take the ten gallons and check back."

"You're a fool to go home now."

"Just get me the gas, Bob."

She went out the front door again to the clatter of the bell, heaved her bags into the passenger seat, and then grabbed two empty gas cans from the back of the truck. She went around the side of the store, her eyes busy, picking out hiding places.

Bob waited for her by the heavy fence that protected the tank.

"It's going to get real rough soon," he said as she handed him the cans.

"Not like it's a surprise."

The stink of diesel filled her nose. She took the full cans and carried them awkwardly to her truck. Bob shadowed her and helped her lift them into the bed. She dug in her pocket for the bills wadded there, but he waved her down.

"I think it's past that, Hannah. If I'm wrong, you can owe me."

She looked aslant at him for a moment, weighing a reply.

"Thanks," she said. "See you later."

It was still morning. Hannah went over her to-do list in her head as she drove the three miles back to the farm.

***

In the summer it was easy to find them. Clouds of fat black flies would gather where they hid. But it was late autumn now, and the flies were gone. Now she would have to draw it out of its hole, make it come to her on her own time. It wouldn't be too hard. These things were scavengers more than hunters. Offer them easy meat and they would always come.

It was morning but the day would draw down quickly now. She unloaded the truck, struggling to haul the gas cans into the shed that housed the generator. She calculated the hours left until full night and measured out the fuel. She made sure she locked the shed door behind her. There were many varieties of scavenger to contend with.

The five dogs still alive barked and chuffed at her, eager to eat and be off their chains. She secured the gate and released them in the yard. They ran and chased each other in spurts but they also stopped and stared out toward the woods across the field, scenting the air. They knew. She filled their bowls and set them down, then went into the house.

It was quiet in the rooms, with the sun slanting through. She unpacked her groceries in the kitchen, putting the narrow selection of canned goods into the cabinets. The last time Bob had gotten a shipment had been in late September. She was lucky there had been anything left to get. Fewer people came in as the year unspooled, gone or dug in where they thought they would be safe. It would be bad when the gardens were completely finished. The first killing frost would come soon. Hunting would never fill in enough. The bullets would run out too. She stopped, sighed, with a box of crackers in her hand.

Everything reaches a tipping point, when what is coming finally overtakes what is. Her eyes burned, and she rubbed them with her wrist. She wanted to be ready.

The dogs were barking again. She looked out the window but couldn't see anything that would provoke them. She knew there was something there, still. It was never far. She let them bark and mill, wearing themselves out while she set the house up for the night. She filled the lamps and moved the bins and furniture from the porch into the kitchen. She secured the extra leashes to the front of the house. At some point in the day, she stopped long enough to make herself a snack. By the time the sun was sliding down the sky, the dogs were tired and lolling along the fence, still watchful.

She called the dogs to her, and they rolled to their feet and trotted to where she stood. Of the pack of brindled mutts, Bucky and Stan were the oldest ones. They were littermates, a gift from her ex-husband when they still thought there was something to save. Stan was getting a little stiff in the hips. She took them both by the collars and led them through the house and into the basement. They didn't understand why they had been suddenly shut in, and whined and scratched at the door. She ignored them, went back out and got the young one, Stevie, and half-carried him in. She had to hold the old dogs back while she wrestled Stevie down the stairs.

The remaining two mutts waited at the kitchen door for her, curious and sheepishly guilty. She tied them up on the porch, patted their heads, got them more food. She looked out past the fence to the treeline, to the shadows stretching out as the day seeped away. She went inside and locked the door behind her, then began the process of shutting up the house for the night.

***

The restlessness and low muttering of the chained dogs woke her from where she slept uncomfortably at the kitchen table. The two kitchen windows were unshuttered, and when she lifted her head she could see a wide swath of the yard under the bluish glare of floodlights. Still groggy, she could not be sure of what was out there. Shadows pooled in too many places. The dogs paced across the porch slowly, aware of something off in the air.

A dark form moved away from anything that would cast it. The dogs froze and bristled. She could hear their hard growling dulled through the glass. She rose slowly and crept along the length of the table. She had lost sight of the figure. She hoped it had not noticed her as she reached for the shotgun propped against the wall. Her fingers closed on the barrel, and she lifted it to hold across her body like a shield. She leaned slowly forward to watch the yard. The dogs ran back and forth on their short chains, growling and snapping, unable to escape.

The generator sputtered and failed. The floodlights faded out, revealing the icy stars. With the hum of electricity stopped, the house filled with silence. She held her breath. In the new darkness, she moved to the window, able to see clearly now into the night. The dogs tied on the porch keened in terror. She watched the shadow figure flow around the side of the house and onto the porch to take its waiting prey, right in front of her. The dog screamed, dying. Deep in the house she could hear the remaining dogs going wild. She ignored them. She raised the shotgun to her shoulder and waited for her shot.

Her motion made her visible, but she did not expect the thing to look back at her, to meet her eyes and see her where she stood. It unfurled from the corpse of the dog and paused there, looking in, as if in some kind of communion with her. She fired.

The wail was thin and choked off as the figure fell. She saw it scramble across the yard, darker than the surrounding night. There was no time to waste now. These things could be cunning. She lit a battery-powered lantern and set about boarding up the shattered window. She did not look at the mangled dog on the porch.

***

The second dog was dead, too, by morning. There was no blood on it. It looked as if it had broken its neck trying to get away. She burned its body with the other. She was tired of this. At least it was only dogs now. It had been so much worse when it was her neighbors.

There was a black track across the dirt where the thing had dragged itself, and a long smear on the fence where it had slithered over. The tall grass on the other side was crushed in a faint trail heading for the trees. Already the grass was beginning to straighten where it had not been snapped. She had no idea how far the thing had travelled, or how close it might be. The threat of nightfall always loomed over her, even as she stood in the sun. She went back to the house.

Only the three dogs in the basement were left alive. She opened the door and they barreled through the kitchen into the yard. They sniffed and whined and pissed on the fence, knowing the other two dogs were gone. She filled their bowls with food and fresh water. She would need them later, when she came back.

Her mouth was dry as she collected supplies for the day. There were too many things she might need. She laid out a lantern, a jar of kerosene, her shotgun. Possibilities opened. She glanced around the kitchen. Water. Matches. A spool of twine. She pulled open her junk drawer and mined it for useful items. The clock above the sink ticked over to 10:14. She added a folding knife to the motley pile and packed up a bag.

***

The day was beautiful, cool with diffuse sunlight. She crossed the field easily along the thing's trail and passed into the company of bare trees. Even in the littered woods the track was clear to read, the ground scraped bare in spots where the thing had stumbled, black fluid from its wound dried into sticky drops on the fallen leaves. There was more of it than she had expected. She walked slowly, casting about for any place where the thing might be hidden. Eventually she realized that the trail had already ended, and there were only the quiet woods around her. She turned to retrace her path, wary of losing her bearings in the newly unfamiliar landscape. She did not have time to wander. It was already after noon.

She focused on finding the end of the trail. Thin sun cut a long shadow, and its shape suggested something more. She turned to it and walked closer.

She did not at once realize that she was looking at the thing's grave. From this angle she could see how the leaf-drift beside a fallen tree was not random, and how the thing had burrowed under it to lay in the place it had died.

Her hand tightened around the shotgun's stock where it hung from her shoulder. She moved toward the mound in measured steps, her breath shallow. Near it, she could smell the sharp tang of spoiled meat. She prodded into the leaves with one booted foot until she felt something solid and soft. Then she kicked at it, connected, heard a rattled cough of expelled air. It did not move. She dropped her knapsack and slung the gun around to her back. She bent and scraped the damp leaves away with her bare hands, exposing the thing's back. It had been a man. His shirt had rutched up beneath him, baring white skin. He stank of old blood. The sweet decay of the leaves could not cover that.

She rolled the body over, saw the messy shotgun wound in his shoulder, looked into his face in the pale light. Her lips quirked before she compressed them in a tight line.

"Peter," she said. "Imagine that."

His eyes drifted open, the corneas faintly milky. He was conscious. She thought that he recognized her. Her chest ached. His mouth moved, too full of teeth. She braced a foot against his ribs and held him down.

"Yes," she said. "Hannah. Imagine that."

Time slipped by around her, but she remained still, above him. She looked into his wide, hungry eyes, waiting for him to come to her. He had been strong and smart, and he had not survived it. Her face felt stiff.

"If I'd have let you in then, we wouldn't be here now," she said to break the ringing silence. He strained upward, weak, wanting. "Ah, well, it has come to this."

She stood up straight and looked around them. Under the bare trees the land rolled gently upward. This is where he had fallen and died. "Not even a cave," she said softly. He had been running away, she thought, away from what was left of the town. Away from anyone he knew. But he hadn't made it far enough. Hunger brought him back. She looked down at him. "Just like you, Peter."

She shifted her weight and stepped away from him. He could reach up but he could not rise under the pressure of the westering sun. That balance would change soon. She looked at her watch. Ten past three. Not much more than an hour of real light left. She wished she had kept better track of it. She had things she still wanted to do.

From the side pocket of the backpack, she fished out a worn claw hammer and a broken-off stool leg. She looked at Peter where he lay, estimating. It wasn't as long as she wanted. It would have to serve for now.

She knelt and drove the makeshift stake through his mangled shoulder, pinning him to the cold ground. He screamed, dull animal sound, and writhed uselessly against it. The meat of his shoulder around the stake was grey and bloodless. She could see down into the layers of fat and muscle, see the dull sheen of bone in the wound. She wondered if it would ever heal.

"Peter," she said, rising to stand over him. He pulled against the stake, trying to escape it. "This is sad."

His hand curled around her ankle, weak, grasping at the leg of her jeans. She bent down to release his grip. He would only get stronger as the night came on. The stake was not long enough to keep him there. Stepping lightly on his wrist, she squatted down close to him. He smelled rotten. She breathed against her sleeve.

"Hannah," he said muddily. "Hannah, let me go."

Her eyes stung with startled tears that she willed dry.

"So you are in there," she said. She could not afford to accept what was left of him. He still leaned up toward her. She met his stare. His eyes were pale green beneath their milky film. There was still light in them.

She was tired. The weight of the last few nights hung like stones on her shoulders.

"Too much even for you," she said. "I thought you would be okay. You're always okay. You piss me off so much."

He watched her, avid. She couldn't read his face. It wasn't really him anymore.

"Hannah," he rasped.

She looked at him, wishing. She knew it was a lie.

"Before I change my mind," she said, and pressed her wrist hard against his parted lips. He closed his mouth against her, turning his face away. She had not expected refusal. He tried uselessly to roll over.

"Come on," she said. "I'm not going to hurt you. This is what you wanted." She shifted her weight against his attempts to throw her off.

Instinct did not own him entirely. As she shoved her wrist against his mouth, he locked his jaws and struggled against her. She straddled him and used the hammer's claw to pry his jaws apart, jamming it back against the corner of his mouth. His lip ripped. She forced the butt of her palm up against his sharp teeth until her skin tore and her blood ran into his mouth. When he tasted it, he lay still beneath her and drank what she gave. She took the hammer away and let him close his mouth around her wrist. It hurt, more than she would have thought. She could feel the poison thrumming up her arm like a spreading infection. At last she pulled her hand away.

"Was that enough to do it, Peter? Is it as simple as that?"

He lay quiet as a waxwork and watched her, licking his teeth, conserving his strength. He twitched against the stake, once, reflex. She looked at her watch again. Nearly four. She could not get back to the house before full dark. Her arm stung. She did not like Peter's eyes on her. She pushed the leaves back over him.

As the light gathered down, she sat against the nearest tree and watched him, thinking. The air was clean here. She breathed deeply. He moved fitfully as the day failed, waking into dusk. The shotgun lay next to her. He was restless enough to dislodge some of the leaves over him. His arm lifted up toward the darkening sky. She rose and retrieved the knapsack. Her head pounded in a dull rhythm, like the first assault of the flu. She wondered how long it would take to happen.

The kerosene sloshed gently as she pulled it out of the bag. There was a crack on the shoulder of the jar but the glass had held. She dug for the matches, satisfied herself that they were dry. Peter had begun to work his way off the stake, arching his back, tearing the wound wider. Night was almost on them.

Her head spun as she went back to where he writhed in the leaves. He looked up at her and growled. Night had finally come, and Peter was gone. She opened the jar and splashed the amber fluid across him. Its heavy chemical tang ruined the cool autumn air. He howled at her, lifting almost clear of the stake as he lunged. She scuffed more debris over him and set a match to the edge of the pile. The leaves smoldered and caught. The smoke was sweet. Bright flame found and followed the ropes of kerosene across the leaves and burned through them, down to Peter's clothes. His shirt caught, then his hair. He screamed and ripped free of his pinning, thrashing, almost strong enough to stand.

She fell back and grabbed the gun and fired at his torso. The shot knocked him back and sprayed bits of burning leaves into the air. Steam streamed from the gaping wound in his belly. He could not get up. She thought his spine might be broken. She slung the gun over her shoulder and scooped up armfuls of forest litter to fuel the fire. It burned through the leaves and twigs quickly.

She stayed within the limits of the firelight and gathered fallen branches to feed to his pyre. Dry bark and wood gave the flames something real to bite, and her skin tightened from the rising heat. Logs crumbled and embers fell, covering him. Peter withered under them, shrinking until he no longer moved or screamed. The only sound now was the crackle of the fire. When she could no longer see him, she went back to sit by the tree, sweating and cold.

Hannah reloaded the shotgun and rested the barrel against her chest. The fire was still bright, but darkness would swallow it soon enough. She was glad the dogs were in the yard. They might have a chance then. Or she would. Her jaw ached. She shifted against the tree, trying to get comfortable. She pulled the gun up higher, tucking it under her chin. She could feel the bones in her face shifting, grinding against each other like boulders. She looked up into the night sky and realized that she could see clearly through the darkness. This was fast. She thought she was ready. As soon as the fire died down, she would finish things. One way or another.

WAITING FOR THE WORMS

THE AIR CONDITIONER rattled heavily in the front window. It was old and noisy, but its compressor kept the worst of the thick July night at bay. Lisa lay on the living room rug with her dirty, bare feet on the lower shelf of the television cabinet, watching *The Goonies* with the sound turned down until it was barely audible over the rumble of the air conditioner. She had seen the movie dozens of times before, two or three times every night since graduation. She alternated it with *Pink Floyd's The Wall*, watching them back to back to back until dawn in search of some kind of equilibrium.

She stared at the screen. Static flickered at the picture's edges and rolled down. The video tape was starting to wear out. She tapped her bare foot against the wooden shelf, unable to keep still.

Ever since her father had sat them down and told her and her older brother about their mother's condition, about her new needs, Lisa had given up sleeping at night. It didn't feel right anymore. Things were different in daylight. Other people were watching then.

So she was nocturnal now. She could watch. She embraced it. There was peace in being the only one awake, and aware. She waited until four thirty each morning to retreat to the room she shared with her two younger sisters, because her older brother got up at five.

In the dark of morning, the bright coral-pink of the walls was muted to a grey she could disregard. She hated the pink walls, and the coordinating floral bedspreads. Lisa had wanted her part of the room to be painted black, but her mother had insisted that it be a feminine room for her three girls. At least she was allowed to hang her Rush posters on her side.

Lisa didn't see her sisters much, despite sharing a room. She would sleep until one or two in the afternoon, then get ready for work at the garden center down the street. She walked back home at nine for a solitary dinner of leftovers or scrambled eggs, and then spent her time in and out of the bathroom until everyone else went to bed. It was the only real privacy she could steal.

A soft, sharp knock on the front door's glass pulled her attention away from the movie. The clock on the VCR said one thirty. One of her friends had to be playing games. She hit the pause button, rolled silently to her feet, and went to the door. The front light was still on, forgotten, burning for the moths. She pulled apart the slats of the blind.

Leaning into the door was Stan, one of her brother's friends. He held up a hand in greeting when he saw her, as if he couldn't gauge the distance between both sides of the door. He motioned for her to let him in.

She had known him forever. He lived at the top of the street, and was always at the house in the daytime, after work. Like her brother, he had picked on her as casual sport for years. She usually ignored him. Fighting back only made the teasing worse.

The door creaked as she pulled it open, tight in its frame. The night air was a wall of humidity that fell into the room.

"Is Donny home?" Stan said. His eyes were very bright. Sweat beaded in his mustache. His long bangs stuck to his damp forehead.

"He's asleep," she said. Stan came in anyway. She knew she shouldn't do it, but she let him.

He wiped his face with his t-shirt and sniffled loudly.

"It's nice in here," he said. "How's your mom doing?"

Lisa shushed him and shook her head.

She led him into the kitchen, where they could talk softly without disturbing her sleeping family. The kitchen had been closed off to make the best use of the air conditioner. The windows were open for whatever breeze might come, but it was oppressively hot. She flicked on the light, and the sudden brightness made them both squint.

"You want me to go get Donny?" she asked.

"Don't wake him up. I didn't come for him," Stan said. "Who else is home?"

"Everyone," she said. She leaned against the counter, neutral.

He pulled a plastic bag out of his jeans pocket.

"Is this okay?" he said. The white powder didn't immediately register with her. Her friends didn't do it. She didn't either. She'd rather drink.

She shrugged.

"Yeah, sure."

"Do you want some?" he asked, holding up the bag.

"No."

He cut the lines of coke on the Formica-topped kitchen table and snorted them up. She watched him clinically, without particular interest. She had seen this in plenty of movies. His eyes lit up again, and he grinned at her. She got a glass of water and sipped at it, ignoring his smile. They were both sweating. The heat hung like a film over them.

Stan wiped at the table with his hand to make sure there was nothing left. She handed him a sponge from the sink, but he waved it away. He licked his fingers. Then he began to speak, low and fast.

"I can't believe how long I've known you. I remember when you were a little girl, and now look at you. You're grown up. You're pretty."

She stayed where she was, watching him over the rim of the water glass.

"I never thought of it before," he said. "But what do you think? You're all grown up now. You used to be such a pest." He laughed at the thought, and came around the table to where she stood.

"What do you think?" he asked again.

She didn't move. She wasn't sure what she should do, what she wanted to do. She'd never thought of Stan like that at all.

He decided for her. He leaned over and kissed her, his mouth too wide over hers. He waggled his tongue in her mouth, searching for hers. She let him. She didn't taste anything. She moved her lips against his in an expected response, but she wasn't there. She didn't think to say no to him. His hands were on her shoulders. He was much bigger than she was, but he was soft. He wouldn't hurt her. She broke the kiss and reached up to take one of his sweaty hands off her, pulling it away.

"Not here," she said. pushing herself away from the counter with her hip. "Someone might come in. Let's go downstairs."

Even though she suggested it, Lisa hated the basement. It was a dim cave under the flat wash of fluorescents, and it smelled of old carpet and mold. More than once her brothers had shut her down there in the dark until she screamed in mortal terror, and kept her trapped until their mother told them to leave her alone. Then she would tell Lisa to stop screaming because it only encouraged them. Right now, though, the basement was cooler, and as far away from the rest of her family as she could get.

And she wasn't alone with what monsters she could imagine.

Stan followed her closely down the stairs, both of them careful to step lightly. She crossed the cluttered main room to the far corner and propped herself against the wall. She let Stan put his arms around her. She didn't care.

"I never thought about it before," he said. "I mean, I thought you were still a little kid. But I looked at you the other day and you were different."

His pupils were huge. He was still sweating, and he smelled of it. Her own perspiration had dried to a tacky film that made her skin drag on the wood-paneled walls when he pressed her back. She let him kiss her again. She wasn't sure how far she was going to go tonight. It didn't really matter.

From upstairs came the sound of a door opening, then footsteps. Stan froze, sudden fear in his face. She recognized the noises of the second-floor bathroom, and the squeak of her oldest brother's bedroom door. Stan shifted his weight to make a space between them.

"Are they coming down?" he whispered near her ear.

She shook her head.

"Maybe this isn't a good idea right now," he whispered again. This time she nodded.

"Wait a minute," she said, and listened for any other sounds above them. Most nights there would be more.

She looked at his eyes as they waited, studying the drug's effect. His irises were a ring of very dark brown around the wide black pupils, visible even as his eyes narrowed against his fear of being caught here with her. He wouldn't look back at her, keeping his line of vision on the wall behind her head.

She wondered what would happen to her if her brother found them there. Or her mother. That would be worse. She wondered what Stan would say then.

Above them, the floor creaked again under uneven footsteps.

"Someone's coming down," Stan whispered. His eyes darted around the basement, looking for a better corner to hide in.

"Let's get out of here," he said, his rough whisper growing louder.

The footsteps stopped. The silence over them was like a held breath.

Lisa slipped out from Stan's forgotten embrace, tugging her t-shirt back into place.

"No. Stay here," she hissed at him. His anxiousness plucked at her nerves.

She went to the foot of the stairs and looked up at the almost-closed door. With a deep sigh, she started back up. She shut the basement door behind her, figuring Stan would be okay for a while.

The living room was empty when she reentered it. The television screen was still frozen on a fuzzy image of a pirate ship on the high seas. She hit the stop button and listened to the VCR whine as it did. She hoped she hadn't ruined the tape.

She went to the stairs and flicked on the upstairs light. She cursed under her breath.

Her mother tottered on the third step down, her long, thin fingers gripping the wallpaper and pulling it loose. Lisa grimaced, disgusted to see her mother's naked body through the flaps of her open robe. Her belly was distended and crossed with scratches. Her skin was as pale and yellowish as paste, sagging slightly from her protruding bones. Lisa didn't want to touch her.

"Go back to bed, Mom," Lisa said, climbing the stairs to stand just below her mother, trying to shoo her up. This close she could not pretend to avoid the smell of old meat, spoiling. The heat hovering at the top of the stairs made it worse. She wondered how her father could stand it.

Her mother looked at her, her runny eyes not focused but seeming to see her daughter anyway. She opened her red mouth and stuttered out sounds around her too-large teeth. There were no words in the jumble. Pink spit dripped from her lower lip.

Lisa grabbed her mother's arms and slowly turned her until she was facing upstairs again. She got behind her ungainly form and nudged her legs up each step until they were both standing in the small hallway. Then she frog-marched her back into her bedroom and wrestled her back into bed.

Her father's side of the bed was empty. The air conditioner was off. The window was open to let the night air in.

"Dad?" she called out, pinning her mother in place.

No one answered.

By the light of the streetlight streaming through the thin curtains, Lisa tucked the sheets securely around her mother and secured the restraints across her chest and legs. Her mother looked toward her in the yellow light, still trying to say something.

Lisa ignored her and made sure the bolt on the outside of the door was secure before she went across to knock at Donny's room. His door bolted on the inside, and she had to wait for him to open it. He took his time.

"C'mon, Donny. I know you were awake a minute ago," she said, leaning into the seam between the door and the frame. She heard him moving around, and rattled the doorknob to hurry him along.

As soon as he opened his door, she made sure he couldn't close it again. Cool air from the room pushed out over her legs.

"Didn't you even hear Mommy getting out?" she said, angry. "And when did Dad go out?"

Donny glared at her.

"He was gone before you even got home tonight."

Lisa stared at him. She hadn't checked before falling into her rut.

"Where?"

"Does it matter?" he asked, trying to shove her out of the doorway. "Mommy's usually quiet anyway."

"Yeah, well, she's not tonight. Did you at least feed her?" Lisa said, pushing back.

Donny dislodged her.

"Nothing to feed her with. That's what Dad went out for."

"Great," Lisa said.

"Go away now. I gotta sleep," Donny said.

"Yeah. Whatever," Lisa said, and let him close his door again. In her parents' bedroom she could hear her mother struggling slowly against the restraints. She was hungry, and she was patient. She would work her way free eventually. Unless her father got back soon with something she would eat, Lisa would have to stay up here and guard the door until he did.

She was sweating again. She went back down to the living room. She wanted a cigarette, even though it was too hot to smoke. Stan was still waiting for her in the basement, but she didn't care. He was stupid to come over and try to move on her. He knew enough about how things were in this house. Donny had told him a plausible story. She wondered what he would do if she told him the whole thing.

That would be funny, she thought. He'd run like Scooby-Doo.

She listened for her mother. Over the noise of the air conditioner, she could just hear her garbled vocalizations. It almost sounded like she was talking, or calling for someone. Lisa shook her head. Her father had said that Mommy remembered talking and taking care of them, but that she didn't remember *them* anymore, not in a way that counted.

And they had to be careful, because without those memories, if Mommy got out, it would be bad.

How bad, he wouldn't say.

She hoped he'd come back soon.

When she thought Donny had gone back to sleep, she snuck back to the basement. Stan was still hanging out in the corner where she'd left him, but he had done more coke while she was gone. He grinned, nervous.

"What's up? I was going to come look for you," he said, remembering this time to keep his voice down. "Everything okay? Everyone asleep?"

"Yeah," she said. Suddenly she was very tired. He was a fool. She would never tell him anything, not even to scare him.

He moved toward her again and tried to put his arms around her. She stopped him, taking a step back, dismissing him with a quick shake of her head.

"Not a good time for this," she said. He looked like a toddler, disappointed. She didn't care. She didn't care about him, or what he expected from her, at all. She wanted this night to be over so she could crawl into her bed and forget it.

Far up in the house she thought she could hear the creak of another floorboard. She hoped it was just the house settling in the heat. It was long past time for Stan to go.

"I think it's safe enough now," she said, and took his hand to lead him back up into the kitchen. He held her hand tightly. At the top of the stairs he turned to push through the swinging door into the dining room, but she stopped him with a tug.

"Back door," she said, letting him stand there, unlocking it and pulling it open. "It doesn't stick as bad."

The storm door was quiet on its hinges. He tried to reach for her as he brushed past her, but she moved away. She put the edge of the door between them, leaning around it. The night air moved slowly around them, heavy and hot. She wanted to shut him out with it already and be done.

"Goodnight," he said as if they had gone on a date. She smiled quickly at him to get him to go. He smiled back and stumbled down the back steps to head around the garage. There was no light in the back yard. He dissolved into the humid darkness.

She pushed the door shut behind him, and for a few seconds stood looking at her hand where it pressed flat on the painted wood. Her fingers were dirty. Her nail polish was chipped. Some prize. She hoped Stan didn't try anything else with her when he was straight again.

She glanced at the clock on the stove. The second hand moved steadily past the red minute hand, but it was only two thirty. It felt like more time had passed. She went back into the living room, glad for the cool air. She hated the heat. She hit rewind on the VCR and lay back down on the floor. The rug was rough under her sticky skin.

From the darkness upstairs she heard her mother groan out another muffled string of not-words, and then the creaking springs of her parents' bed. It sounded like her mother had begun to work the restraints loose again.

She figured she still had some time. Her mother was clumsy and slow. It's not like she could ever get hurt, or starve to death.

If she could, they would all be free.

Outside, she heard the familiar sound of the family car pulling up in front of the house. Her father was finally home. She hoped he had found enough for a few days this time.

With her feet propped up on the television cabinet, she waited through the click and hiss of the VCR for the familiar movie to start again.

TO DIE, TO SLEEP, NO MORE

REPORTS OF A new plague had begun a little less than a year before, scattered through Europe and Asia. And then, like a wave crashing, the sickness was everywhere. Travel bans and quarantines didn't stop it. Health care systems collapsed as it swept through, overwhelmed by its ferocity.

It started with a sudden fever, a wracking wet cough. Then came a searing headache, bloodshot eyes, cramps, hemorrhage, organ failure. The CDC said it was certainly transmitted by close contact, but it had spread to so many, so fast, it must also be airborne. So far, it had killed nearly eighty percent of those infected. Many people called it simply the flu, knowing it wasn't. But it was easier than calling it a plague.

"Laura's mother says it came from the Israelis. A bioweapon. They made it look like Iran was behind it," Corry said.

"Laura's mother is nuts," Tom said. "And Laura's not far behind her."

"Then how did it start?" Corry asked, her voice rising.

Tom slammed the drawer shut and leaned against the counter. He wouldn't look at her. He drew a deep breath before he answered. "They don't know. Not yet, at any rate. Maybe when it's run its course and people develop some immunity they'll have time to figure it out."

"*We* don't have time," Corry said.

Tom grunted, but wouldn't look at her. "Maybe it's our punishment," he said.

When he began to cough, Corry walked away. She needed to check on Ruby again.

***

The city changed as the plague swept through that winter. Hospitals had stopped taking in patients weeks ago as their staffs died along with the plague's other victims. The ugly, too-sweet stink of rotten meat lingered now in pockets where no one had come to bury the bodies. What was left of the government concentrated its depleted resources on the living. The dark ages had returned.

Corry wondered only briefly about how quickly it had all fallen apart. It didn't really matter now.

She filled a bowl with water and rubbing alcohol, and listened as Ruby struggled to breathe.

Tom had set up a cot for the girl on the tiny sunporch off the kitchen so they could keep a close watch over her. Corry squeezed into the narrow space and knelt beside her daughter. She wiped Ruby's face and neck gently with a wet cloth, trying to cool her fever. The sharp smell of the alcohol cut through the sick-room stink for a moment before it evaporated.

"Mommy," Ruby mumbled, half-awake.

Beneath the flush of fever, Ruby's skin had faded to a yellowish pallor, her cheeks and eyes sunken, the curves and angles of her small skull pushing up like a mask. Corry was careful, afraid of ripping the girl's fragile skin.

Then she dipped the cloth in the bowl again and ran it over her own face. She shivered, and she burned.

***

People in the streets wore surgical masks and disposable gloves. Some carried spray bottles of bleach with them. Some carried amulets they had made or bought, designed to ward away evil. Each day there were fewer people out, as they hid or sickened and died. Corry wondered how far faith could carry them now.

She jumped when she heard the front door bang shut. She had fallen asleep next to Ruby.

"Tom?" she called out, struggling to stand on numb legs.

"It's just me," he said, and coughed.

"Did you go out?" she said, limping into the kitchen as he walked in.

"I heard about something," he said. He carried an old baby food jar full of a thick black liquid, a larger jar of what looked like olive oil, and a photocopied list of instructions.

"What is all that?" Corry said, reaching for the jars. Tom kept them away from her, placing them gently on the kitchen counter. From his pocket he pulled a third jar, empty and clean.

"You have no idea how much these cost," he said. His voice was thick with phlegm. "But if they work, it doesn't matter."

Corry picked up the baby food jar. It was hot to the touch.

"But what is it? Where did you get it?"

"Benny's wife. She's a botanist. She's been trying to find some kind of remedy for the flu, and she's pretty sure this will do it."

Tom shook his head, looking past Corry.

"Pretty sure. She said it showed some effect when she gave it to her dog. It's not a cure. But maybe."

Corry picked up the instruction sheet and read over it.

"This isn't botany," she said. "This looks like voodoo magic."

Tom shrugged. "It probably is. At this point, what would it hurt?"

Corry put the paper down beside the jars and smoothed it flat. She shook her head, unable to give any real reason it would.

"I think we've all gone mad," she said.

***

Tom wasn't there when Ruby finally died.

He couldn't take the girl's suffering, or Corry's dull recounting of Laura's theories on the plague.

"That woman is nuts, and you're nuts for even listening to her," he had said.

Maybe I am, Corry thought. Maybe you are, with your potions. Maybe it doesn't matter.

What mattered was Ruby, and her life sputtering out.

Tom went over the directions with Corry, taking turns reading them aloud until they were both sure of the sequence. She didn't bother to disagree with his magical thinking. It gave him some comfort. That might be all this was worth.

He laid the jars out on a clean cloth on the sunporch floor where Corry would be able to reach them easily. He kissed Corry, and kissed Ruby. He held Ruby's hot, boneless hand for a long while, watching her fail. Then he went to sit on the front porch, unable to see the task through.

Corry crouched alone at her daughter's bedside with the empty jar pressed to Ruby's mouth to catch her final breath. She knew it wouldn't be much longer. Her fingers were clumsy. The jar opening kept slipping down over Ruby's tiny chin. Corry listened to the death rattle buzzing in her daughter's throat and tried to keep from crying.

When the rattle stopped, Corry held her own breath to listen to the silence. She kept the jar in place, examining Ruby's face for any sign of life. But she was gone.

Corry slid the jar carefully off her daughter's mouth. She capped the jar tightly, her hands shaking, and put it aside to ready the rest. She willed herself not to cry.

Following the instructions, she rubbed oil into Ruby's skin, through her hair, into the secret places of her body. She dipped a sponge into the black fluid and swabbed Ruby's mouth with it, then poured a thin sticky stream into her dull half-lidded eyes. She arranged Ruby's body neatly on the bed, pulling the covers back. How thin Ruby had become with this sickness riding her. She had been such a healthy girl before.

Corry broke and sobbed tearlessly, but quickly stifled herself. She picked up the jar that had caught Ruby's last breath. She bit into her tongue and the inside of her cheek, hard, and when she tasted blood she opened the jar and spat into it. Then she added more black fluid, enough to pour, and swirled it until it mixed.

She slipped a hand behind Ruby's neck and lifted her head, then tipped the jar up against her lips. The fluid ran out at the corners of the girl's slack mouth. Corry laid her flat again, hoping enough had run down her throat.

Corry floated between hope and despair. She wasn't sure how long this should take, or what it would look like if it happened. If it *could* happen. If she wasn't trying to convince herself to deny the inevitable.

She kept busy. She lined the jars up neatly on their cloth, capping the oil and the black fluid. She wondered if she should wash out the other one. She wondered if she should go get Tom. She wiped a streak of red from Ruby's cheek.

Then she waited.

***

Some time later, Tom came back in, coughing. Corry didn't move. She kept her eyes on Ruby. She believed she had seen a tremor move across the girl's body, like a ripple in water. She wanted to see it again.

"Did you finish?" Tom said, leaning into the porch.

"Shh. Yes," Corry whispered. She glanced up at Tom. He looked bad. His face was sallow, with deep creases around his mouth. He tried to swallow another cough. Ruby's body trembled again.

"Did you see that?" Tom hissed. "What's happening?"

"I don't know," Corry said.

He pushed into the narrow space beside the bed, shoulder to shoulder with Corry.

"Is it working? Are you sure you did it right?" he said, grabbing her arm, squeezing it too tightly. His hand was hot. She shrugged away.

"I did exactly as you told me," Corry said, watching Ruby's body twitch and jerk.

"It looks like it hurts," he said.

Corry didn't answer him. She didn't want to think about any more pain.

She stroked Ruby's dirty hair, smoothing the dark strands around the girl's withered face. For a moment the tremors stopped, and Ruby lay still. Then the empty body spasmed, bent, and almost sat up before falling back.

Ruby gasped, a terrible, hollow sound with no breath behind it. Her mouth moved.

"Mommy," she said in a dry, unfamiliar voice. "I want my mommy."

Corry screamed and fell back, but Tom leaned forward toward his struggling daughter.

"She's back," he said, his voice rising. Anything else he tried to say was lost in a coughing fit.

***

Corry lost track of the days after Ruby came back. Tom came and went, coughing, struggling. Sometimes she heard him in the yard working. Then Corry lost track of him as well.

She went as far as the front steps to look for him once, and found that a cool, damp spring had finally come.

A flyer was stuck into the screen door handle. She glanced at the houses across the street. Flyers had been left on them too. More copies blew down the street and across lawns. She pulled the paper loose and read its bolded, all-caps message.

THE ANSWER TO YOUR PRAYERS IS HERE, it said. THE DOCTORS DON'T KNOW BUT I DO. Then it listed a phone number for more information.

Corry wanted to laugh at the idiot simplicity of it. Whoever had strewn the flyers about had no idea. There were no prayers to answer anymore.

***

"I'm scared of her," Tom said one day, breathless and weak. Corry stared at him, flatly.

"It's too late for that now," she said. "This is what you wanted."

"Not this," he said. "Not this."

But Corry was trapped in the ritual, responsible for what they had done. She burned sage and anointed her daughter every day, rubbing the oil into Ruby's cold skin, swabbing Ruby's slack mouth with the black potion, dropping it into her filmy eyes.

"I want my mommy," Ruby said, the words slurred on the grey meat of her tongue.

Corry's skin burned now. The pain behind her eyes swelled until her vision was a narrow band. Sometimes Corry remembered to eat. Sometimes she forgot, because Ruby never needed to eat. Ruby never needed to sleep. Corry tended her daughter according to the photocopied instructions, but what Ruby needed was beyond what Corry could give.

Tom left. She heard him rattling tools in the garage. He did not come back.

***

Ruby stood beside Corry's bed like a carving, like a broken stick. There was no life in her wasted body. She decayed, despite the oil and the black fluid. Her blank presence was a drain, unanswerable.

"I want my mommy," the dead girl whined in a voice like wind over long grass.

Corry sat up and reached out to stroke her daughter's cold face. She was alone.

"It's okay, baby. I'm right here."

"I want my mommy," Ruby said again. And again. And again. The dead girl repeated her plea every few seconds like a metronome.

"Ruby, I'm here," Corry said. She nudged her daughter back from the edge of the bed so she could get up.

"I want my mommy," Ruby said. Her glazed eyes focused on nothing. Her tone didn't change.

Corry wiped at her own sweaty face. Her bones hurt. She wanted to sleep.

"Come here, baby," she said.

Ruby followed her stiffly into the kitchen. Corry dug through a drawer until she found the duct tape.

"I want my mommy," Ruby said.

"Hush now," Corry said, and sealed her mouth.

Ruby's clouded eyes still stared, and her rotten jaw still moved, but no voice came through the tape. Corry smiled, patting Ruby's softening head.

"Good girl," she said.

***

As the sun rose, Corry laid out the jars as she had done every morning since the first, following the ritual.

She rubbed the oil into Ruby's slipping skin, cringing as the tissues shifted under her hands. She loosened the tape around the dead child's moving mouth, but it stuck to the withered flesh and left Ruby's lip hanging like a torn hem. Corry screamed and burst into tears.

Ruby's thin, raspy voice spilled out, unintelligible now but making the same demand. Corry cried with messy sobs, steeled herself, and swabbed Ruby's ripped, rotten mouth. Her touch dislodged most of the baby teeth from the slushy gums.

She stopped, helpless against the drag of dissolution. Ruby made her noises, needy and inconsolable.

Corry struggled to breathe as she coughed, sudden and deep, her throat full of mucus. She forced herself to the kitchen sink, poured out what was left in the jars, and spat into the mess as she washed it down the drain.

***

Tom had died in the yard near a grave he had dug for Ruby. She remembered now. He had given up on the ritual, the resurrection. She had lost track.

Corry rolled his body into the small hole. It didn't fit. She didn't care. She could barely focus through the pain inside her eyes and the throbbing ache in her joints and her belly. She scraped dirt over Tom's wasted body with her bare hands. This was the best she could do for him.

Behind her, Corry heard the drag of Ruby's footsteps coming over the lawn. Her daughter's stench enveloped her as Ruby came to stand at her shoulder.

"I want my mommy," Ruby almost wheezed. There was not enough flesh left in her mouth and throat to form the words, but Corry could fill in the gaps. She turned on her knees to look at the remains of her daughter. Ruby's bare jaw still worked to speak her need. It would never stop.

Corry looked away. Her head felt as if it would crack open. Her vision dimmed. She lowered herself onto the cool dirt of her husband's grave and closed her eyes.

Above her, Ruby stood like a broken branch driven into the earth, the shreds of her voice begging, and begging, and begging.

OUT WITH THE OLD

OUTSIDE, THE COLD night was broken with fireworks and bursts of laughter from the streets below.

"Have to see the New Year," the old woman gasped. "Have to."

"Quiet, Annie," Jess said, smoothing the bedsheets over her new patient.

The old woman's skin was like marble. She wouldn't last much longer.

Jess might still make the party.

Jess startled when Annie grabbed her wrist and pulled her close.

"Can't go yet," Annie rasped.

Jess could hear the rattle behind her words.

"Stop that," Jess said sharply, tugging loose. She glanced at the window as she filled the syringe. Bright music filled the room despite the glass.

"How soon?" Annie coughed.

"Soon," Jess said. She looked at the clock over the bed. "Ten minutes."

"Have to see," Annie wheezed. Her eyes were not quite closed. A thin rim of white showed through her sparse lashes.

"You will," Jess murmured, and sank the needle into Annie's arm. She depressed the plunger slowly, watching Annie's face fall slack as the morphine did its work. Annie's breathing slowed, stopped.

Jess glanced at the clock. Eleven fifty-eight.

Close enough, she thought.

The celebration outside grew louder with noisemakers and cheers. Jess pressed Annie's eyes shut and drew the sheet over her face. She heard the countdown reach its end, and over it the thin wail of a hungry baby.

Then she heard nothing.

Uneasy, she raised the window. Outside was silent, starless and dark.

There was no celebration.

There was nothing at all.

WORLD ENOUGH, AND TIME

"SHE'S A CANCER," Terry said, exhaling a stream of blue vapor into the sharp-edged cone of light shining up from their tiny table. Terry had begun speculating as soon as he had seen her stroll into the café. It was his way of making conversation.

"Really," Pat said with studied boredom.

"Of course she is. Look at her skin."

Terry was not to be dissuaded. Pat turned slowly on his chair to better observe the woman in question. She sat at the front of the café, staring over her coffee at her own reflection in the plate glass window. Everything about her was smooth—her glossy skin, her slicked-back hair, the seamless grey tunic and leggings outfit that skimmed her thin frame. He studied her, lured by something familiar about her. She caught Pat watching her in the glass, made eye contact with his reflection, smiled at him thinly and without humor until he turned back to Terry.

"Well, she's rich," Pat said, slurping at his cup of now-tepid tea to hide his discomfort.

"They all are," Terry said. "But look at her. It's like she never lived a day."

"You act like you've never seen one."

"Not this close. Neither have you. I'm telling you, she looks like she's been dipped in wax."

Pat waited before turning again. The woman immediately saw his motion in the window. She raised her hand and gestured for him to come to her.

"Looks like I'm up," Pat said to Terry, pushing back his seat. He threaded his way between the tiny, crowded tables to present himself.

"It is you," she said, a warm smile on her painted mouth.

"Maria?" he said. "Oh my god, I almost didn't recognize you! How are you?"

"I'm good," she said. Even her voice was polished, without any remnant of regional accent.

"Please. Sit," she said, tilting her head toward the chair beside her. Pat sat down gingerly. This close, the woman was unnerving. Cellular immortality had given her the glib sheen of a mannequin. When she extended her hand to him, he paused before shaking it.

"Please. Sit," she said again.

He sat.

"I wasn't entirely sure it was you," she said.

"Oh, it's me," Pat said with a sudden grin. She made him nervous. "I just didn't expect it to be you. How long has it been?"

Pat already knew. He remembered her from sophomore year in high school, before his family moved and he had to transfer. They had been friends for a while. He had crushed on her, hard, had even believed he loved her, but had never asked her out.

"Wow, it has to be, what, twenty-six years?" she said.

"I think so," he answered.

"Yeah. You moved away in tenth grade. I remember. So, how did you end up back here?"

Pat didn't respond at first. He waved a waiter over and ordered a hot black tea, buying time to summarize the last few decades.

"My parents split up during my freshman year at college. Mom came back here, so I did too. Never made it out again. What about you?"

"I'm back for a longish visit. My sister's still here"

"A lot has changed."

"Yes," she said. "I think the last time I was here was about six years ago. Then my parents moved to the Carolinas and there wasn't much reason to come back."

She rattled her spoon against the tabletop.

"I got divorced a couple of years ago. He was a jerk. But they all are, after it's done." She sipped quickly at her cold coffee. "Anyway, I did just fine in the settlement. Now I get to travel."

Pat looked at her for guidance. She laughed. "That was a joke."

"Yeah," he said.

"How about you?" she said, still with a laugh in her voice to cover the awkwardness. "What's your story?"

"You know. Never married, never left. I do freelance content for any site that will have me. It's a living."

Pat noticed Terry cutting between the tables to join them. He had been gone longer than he thought.

"Maria, this is my friend Terry," Pat said as Terry reached them, wrapping himself in social convention. "Hey, Terry," he said. "Maria and I went to high school together for a while. Saint Paul's. Until tenth grade, anyway. I think that's why she noticed me at all. I didn't recognize her, not after..."

He trailed off, knowing he had wandered into judgement and insult, however unintended.

Maria had begun to shred her napkin, obviously nervous and trying to cover it with action.

Terry held out his hand to her. "Hi," he said. "Pat's mentioned you before."

"Pat," she said at last. "Yes. We were in Durzik's class together."

"Yes," Pat said, after a long pause. "I hated literature because of her."

"She wasn't so bad," Maria said, stronger now, bantering. "Not like gym with Palletti."

"Right," Pat said. He glanced up at Terry. "Why don't you sit?" he said.

"Actually, I have to go," Maria said. She took out her wallet and laid too many bills on the table.

"You don't have to do that," Pat said.

She kept her hand over the money, her eyes confused.

"No, it's okay," she said. "I have money."

"Thanks," he said.

She fumbled the wallet back into her purse, pushed her chair back.

"It was great to see you. Oh, and before I go, what's your number?" She wiggled her phone in her hand and smiled.

Pat gave it to her, and saved hers when she tapped it in and called him.

"I'll be in town for a couple of weeks, at least," she said. "I'll call you."

Pat smiled back at her as she walked away from them. He examined the number on the screen as if looking for a hidden meaning.

Terry watched her leave the café before turning back to Pat.

"She's way off," he said.

"What do you mean?"

"You saw it. She was having a hard time tracking both of us. It was like it was too much for her to process."

"Maybe."

Terry slid his chair back, ready to leave.

"She is pretty."

***

His phone chirped. Maria, at last. He closed the article he was working on. It wasn't coming together anyway.

Hey. You free tonight?
Yes. What do you want to do?
Who is this?
Pat.
Pat who?
Pat Mikelson.
How did you get my number?
Maria, are you okay? You just messaged me.
Stop messaging me.
I'm going to call you now.

He thumbed down to her number and tapped it. Her phone rang until it went to voicemail. He dialed again. She answered.

"Hey, Pat. I was just thinking about you."

His mouth tasted sour. She was one of those, he realized, one of the unfortunate cancers whose wonderful new cells had infected her brain. Timeless, they replaced existing tissue and created shards of progressively more disconnected memories with nothing to link one to another.

He had read the investigative articles about the phenomena, the long eulogies to the eternally young already lost to regenerative technology. Once the potential for damage was known, the treatments went off-shore. Clean, expensive clinics opened in warm vacation spots with lax medical standard enforcement, and stem cell infusion became a popular experiment for the rich and insecure. It was still heavily advertised, if one knew where to look. There was too much money to be made, too much youth to be regained for anything as disposable as memory and self to take precedence.

"That's a fine coincidence," he said. "I was thinking about you too."

***

They met in the park for lunch, the chill of early spring a relief after grey winter. Sitting on a bench in the bright daylight, he studied her face between mouthfuls of cheese sandwich. Her skin was unmarked, like poured milk. Her brows and lashes were glossy. Even her teeth were immaculate. But her bone structure, the fat under her flawless skin, the shape and hang of her muscles, were all those of a mature woman. He looked down at where she held her sandwich in its foil and catalogued the differences between his weathered hand and her pristine one.

They met often, in the park. She was as alien as the new growth of spring herself. He enjoyed the novelty. Her dissonance was still intriguing.

***

"I think I'm falling in love with you, Maria," Pat said, embracing her as they waited for the movie to load. It wasn't strictly true. He was falling in love with the increasingly blank slate of her.

She smiled. Clarity wavered in her eyes, becoming confusion.

"Do you love me?" he said, prompting.

She looked down, still smiling. Her voice was light and artificially careless as she said, "I do for now!"

Pat released his hold on her shoulders and moved away from her.

"What's my name?" he said, frustrated by her lapses. They were coming more frequently as the days passed. A cold spot grew in his chest.

Maria twisted like a squirming child.

"Oh, don't be so silly!" she cried. "Of course I know your name. I said I love you, didn't I?"

Pat pulled her against him again, rubbing her narrow back mechanically. She remained tense, ready to leap away from him.

He slid his hand around her waist, trying to change his mood, until he was brought up short by the small plastic rectangle taped to her skin. He fiddled with it, curious, before she brushed his fingers away.

"Don't touch it," she said. "You'll mess with the settings."

Wherever her mind had been, she was back.

"What is it?"

"It controls the renewal cells. Hormones, enzymes, chemo. A little bit of everything."

She lifted her shirt to show him the thin line running from the pump to the indwelling subcutaneous port. "It's modeled after an insulin pump," she said.

"How long do you have to wear it?" he asked.

She glanced at him sidelong, as if measuring his sincerity. "Always," she said at last. "Like with transplant drugs."

"What happens if you stop?" he said, his fingers still tracing the pump's outline.

She looked at him, gauging his intent. "Nothing, at first. But with nothing to stop the cell division, it turns into cancer pretty quickly."

"And why did you do something like this?" His tone was sharper than he'd meant it to be.

"Because I wanted to," she said, standing up. She was flustered, suddenly defensive. "I think I would rather spend the night by myself if you don't mind."

His temper rose but he measured his words.

"Maria, I'm sorry. I didn't mean anything."

"Everyone means something. You think I don't know what people think of me?"

"Cancers. That's what people think of you."

Her face hardened to a mask.

"Don't call me that. It's ugly."

Pat shrugged, a reptilian part of him wanting to be ugly.

"You're not stupid. You know that cancer has nothing to do with the process," she said.

He wouldn't let it go. "It's not the process. It's the way you are."

Maria stood up and walked to the window. Her shoulders were stiff.

"I'll call you if I want to see you again, Pat. You know your way out."

***

Maria called. She always called, losing the thread of any argument. She remembered him, most of the time. And Pat answered, because he did in his way love her.

But he did not enjoy it. In person, Maria was an uncomfortable presence, her perpetual newness a reminder of how she had tried to shed mortality. She no longer looked truly human, instead resembling an exquisite doll. Pat disliked going out with her, dreading the stares she drew, and the moment that came in every outing when her memory stuttered and she became afraid. Sometimes she was lucid enough to explain it. She said it felt like remembering déjà vu without ever having the original experience of it. He couldn't fathom what she described. He often grew impatient with her. But he answered.

***

Terry chewed his bagel slowly as Pat explained.

"Clinics in Mexico were doing this almost as soon as it was discovered. Nobody was dying from it. Not yet. But nobody knew what could happen either. Oh, yeah, they suspected there would be an increase in cancer from it—let's face it, if the cells weren't modulated they would *be* cancer. And the cancer rate did skyrocket, aggressive cancers that didn't respond to surgery or targeted therapies. The unexpected side effect was the dementia.

"Some of the immortal cells they seeded her with...metastasized, colonized, her brain. It happens, sometimes, with the procedure. Hit or miss. Now there are lesions on her brain that can be treated but not eliminated, and new cells are growing there as well. Her memory is a mess. They haven't figured out how to stop it."

Terry finished eating before he responded.

"She's creepy, Pat. She's like that actress, the one who was big in the nineties. After she became a cancer she got really loopy until she stopped going out in public. That's what Maria's like."

"Shut up, Terry."

"No, you know I'm right." He wiped his fingers. "You need to decide how far you are going to let yourself be dragged down."

***

"When will Pat be back?" Maria said. Her voice trembled. Terry couldn't judge how well her mind was working behind her fever-bright eyes.

"Maybe half an hour. Do you want something to drink?"

She shook her head sharply, as if there were something buzzing in her ear.

"I know you don't like me," she said. "You don't want Pat to get hurt, and I can't help but hurt him."

Terry sipped at his beer. "It's more complicated than that, Maria. You know that."

"Yes. I know that."

She sat down, tucked her legs under her on the couch. "He's always been a good person," she said. "Even in high school, he was honest and truly nice. You can't imagine how glad I was to run into him again after so many years."

Terry walked slowly past her to the window, pushed aside the curtains to watch the traffic below them. She did not turn.

"I love him, Terry."

Terry leaned his head on the glass.

"You can't count on that," he said. "Not with what's happening to you."

"That's not fair. You don't get to make the call."

"No," he said. "No, I don't. But I do get to register my opinion. You are going to hurt him very badly. I will be there for him when you can't be anymore. He's got that. You don't."

Terry turned to face her, although she resolutely kept her back to him.

"I think you're a good person too, Maria. I actually like you a great deal. I think if things had gone another way, you would be very good for Pat. I'm jealous of what could have been with you two. But the reality is that as much as he thinks he will, he will not be there for you. Nice guy, but he doesn't have it in him."

Maria's head dropped, her sleek hair falling in a wave.

"It's not fair," she said, but her voice was fading.

***

"Where's Cathy, Maria?" Dr. Redfield asked while glancing over her notes.

"Cathy?"

"Your sister Cathy. You have her listed as your support person."

"Oh," Maria said, her voice flat. "She couldn't come."

Dr. Redfield put her tablet down and took Maria's jaw in her gloved hand.

"Open wide, dear," she said, and quickly swabbed Maria's cheek when she obeyed.

She wiped the swab onto a film and ran it through the scanner. In a few minutes the computer pinged and transmitted the results to the printer. Redfield loaded a set of empty cartridges and set the printer to fill them.

"How long will these last her?" Pat asked.

"You're her keeper now?"

"I think so."

"About a week each," Redfield said colorlessly, her eyes on the machinery. "The pump has an alert on it that goes off twelve hours in advance of running empty."

"Okay," Pat said.

"Do you know her sister?"

"No."

"Remind me to give you her number."

Redfield examined Maria quickly, pressing on the lymph nodes in her throat, armpits, and groin before listening to her lungs. Maria sat like a child with her hands in her lap, passive, too shy to express any displeasure with her doctor.

"She's not due for another MRI yet, but make sure she keeps the next appointment. Once the brain is affected, the chance of cancers developing goes up very quickly."

"Can you tell me how long ago she had this done?"

Redfield tapped the screen. "Four years," she said. "She was one of the earlier ones.

"They go down to Mexico looking for these miracles, and they end up like Maria, or worse. The clinics down there don't care about outcomes, because they aren't cleaning up the mess."

"How many patients like her do you treat?"

Redfield gave a short bark of laughter. "Too many. I'm only a boutique service. The big centers and the in-hospital clinics do most of the regular maintenance for the fountain of youth brigade."

Pat helped Maria into her jacket. She still was not present. Redfield watched him.

"How much do you know about the process? What Maria underwent?"

He steered Maria into a chair. She sat placidly, examining her fingers. He hoped her mind would click back into place soon.

"Some."

"All right," Redfield said. "The short version is this: Directed differentiation of cloned and immortalized stem cells—not cancer cells, only a cancer cell's infinite telomeric replication—allows endless renewal, endless cellular replication. The original body becomes its own scaffold for the new cells as the senescent cells age and die. The body will not age, not in any way we would define it. Effectively immortal. However, the immortal cells are also prone to tumor formation unless constantly regulated by suppressive chemotherapy and hormonal controls."

She paused to breathe and make a few notes.

"That's where I come in, because it's too much trouble to transport medicinal drugs illegally across international borders."

Pat nodded.

"Look," Redfield said. "All I ask is that you don't dump her. Call me if you're going to bail so I can follow up."

Pat blinked at her, suddenly aware of the pressure.

Then Maria stood up and smoothed her pants across her hips.

"Hi, Dr. Redfield. How are you?"

***

Pat scrolled through Maria's phone. She watched a sitcom in silence as he did. He didn't think she knew what it was. The number he wanted was saved under Clínica de la Restauración, the name so obvious as to be sarcastic.

"So, call," Terry said.

Pat called.

The ringing sounded tinny, as if it were running through old wires. After eight rings the call connected, but no one spoke.

"Hello?" he said to the empty air. "Is this the clinic?"

"Who is calling?" came a smooth voice, female and American.

"I'm calling for Maria Tarnowski," Pat said. "She was there four years ago for your treatment. I need to know what cell line was used. She's having a bad response and we need to fight it."

The open connection buzzed like distant locusts.

"I'm sorry," the American voice said. "I wish I could help you, but we've only been open since December."

And then she ended the call.

He looked at the blank screen for a minute before unlocking it and scrolling up to Cathy's contact information. He tapped it. The dissonant tones of a bad number chattered in his ear.

Pat pressed the phone back into Maria's limp hand and looked at Terry. He shrugged.

***

"Pat," Terry said, "you're making a mistake with her. There's too much not right with Maria, and it's going to bury you at some point."

"I think you're wrong," Pat said.

Terry leaned against the counter. "Of course you do. You love her. She's a nice person. But she's not going to stay a nice person. She's not going to stay even a person."

"Stop it."

"What are you going to do when she forgets you?"

Pat looked at him, unable at first to respond. His lips twitched. "Go to Mexico, I guess," he said.

***

"Terry?"

"Yeah, man."

"It happened."

"What do you mean? Is she dead?"

"No." Terry could hear Pat start to choke and cry. "She's just breathing. The Maria part is gone."

"I'll be right there."

Pat buzzed him in when he rang. There was no one in the lobby or the elevator. He felt like a ghost going down the hall to Maria's apartment. Pat was waiting with the door ajar.

"Where is she?" Terry said, clutching his friend's hand.

Pat pointed toward the bedroom. He stayed in the foyer while Terry went to see.

Maria was in the rocking chair between the bed and the window, swaddled in blankets and watching the sky. Her eyes passed over Terry as he walked in, but rolled back to the blue expanse without recognition. Her face was blank and peaceful, like a wax figure. She seemed alive, but at this point it was a technicality. He tasted bile behind his teeth.

He went to her, felt her smooth cheek for fever.

"Are you hungry?" he asked her. She didn't respond.

"Maria?"

She only looked at the sky. Terry picked her phone up from the bedside table. It wasn't locked. He scrolled until he recognized the name Pat had mentioned, dialed it.

"Dr. Redfield's office."

"Maria Tarnowski needs an ambulance," he said.

"I'm sorry? If this is an emergency, you need to call 911."

"But I'm calling you. Maria Tarnowski, 778 Barrens Avenue, apartment 9C. She needs an ambulance. Thank you."

He hung up and walked back to where Pat waited.

"What do you have here?"

"What?"

"Clothes, stuff. What's here?"

"Nothing. Nothing."

"Good. Let's go."

Terry pulled Pat out of the apartment, making sure the door locked behind them.

"There's nothing to save. The only thing that can happen now is we get blamed for something."

Pat stopped at the elevator. Terry pressed the lighted button and watched the floor numbers glow in their turn. The elevator chimed as the car reached their floor. When the doors slid open, the men stepped in and let the car carry them down.

SOMETHING AFTER

FELICE GAZED UP at the front of her father's house. It was dingier than she remembered it, the brick front eroded, the landscaping overgrown, the lawn gone to seed. She sighed. At least it was still almost as big as it had seemed in her childhood. She could just barely remember when they had first moved in, the surprise of it after the limits of the apartment. It had been vast then, and unexplored.

A shadow crossed one of the wide picture windows that flanked the front door. Amira had beat her here, despite her reluctance to come. Felice looked around for her sister's car, but didn't see it. She pulled out her phone and scrolled through for Amira's number, but she didn't see it. She scrolled again. She didn't remember deleting it.

Amira was always just beyond her reach.

She tried the number for her father's old landline. The grating mechanical pulse meant a receiver was off the hook somewhere. It didn't surprise her. There had been no one to answer it for weeks. Not since he had died. She drew a deep, shuddering breath, refusing to cry.

Felice knocked to warn Amira, then let herself in. Her own shadow stretched in a long band before her, until she shut the door against the light.

"Hello?" she called into the stillness.

"Back here," Amira answered. "In his office."

Felice shrugged out of her coat as she walked down the long hallway. Of course that was where she would be.

***

He was still here, somewhere. She knew it.

Felice ran her hands over the damp, papered walls of the old office, spreading her arms wide until her cheek pressed the brighter spot where a picture had once hung. She closed her eyes, imagining the room as it had been when he was here, furnished and cluttered with work, and with life.

She stepped back from the wall and opened her eyes.

The thin sunlight seeping in through the high windows made the room seem even emptier than it was. The dulled Persian carpet was pitted where chair legs had rested too long without moving, and the scattered scorch marks before the fireplace were too many to be hidden by the pattern. The only piece of furniture remaining was his desk.

"Well?" Amira asked.

Felice shook her head, coming back from her reverie. "I smell him," she said. "His cigarettes."

Amira moved slowly toward the door. "It's just your memory," she said from the threshold. "It smells of nothing but mold and dust in here."

Felice smiled thinly. "My memory," she said quietly. "What else could it be, but memory?"

Amira watched her sister closely for a moment, her eyes narrowed.

"I'll leave you to it then," she said at last, and swept away down the hall.

***

The desk's dark wood was mazed with scratches and scarred with years of cigarette burns. Felice pulled open one of the drawers. The faint smell of rubber erasers drifted up. She remembered how fascinating the soft, kneaded erasers had been to her when she was small, how much she liked to play with them instead of plain clay.

She reached up to touch the scar above her left eye, a souvenir of when she had run into the sharp edge of her father's drafting T-square when she was two. She couldn't remember it happening, but she knew the well-worn family story.

She remembered how he said she had screamed and screamed.

***

Upstairs in their father's room, Amira stood amidst the piles of his possessions, sorted into what might be worth something and what was pure junk. It was the last room to clear out, the last of what was left of him. Felice could not stop touching the pile of discards, picking up worn belts, old ties, half-used bottles of aftershave.

"This is your inheritance," Amira said, her jaw clenched around the words. "His leavings, all for nothing."

"Don't you miss him?" Felice asked, surprised at Amira's anger.

Amira braced her feet, as if she leaned into a heavy wind.

"No," she said. "Not after, I don't."

Felice put down the shirt she held and looked away. She didn't want to remember.

"I miss him," she said to her sister's silence.

***

As Felice bent over the sink to brush her teeth, she caught a sideways glimpse of a figure passing the open doorway. She spat out the toothpaste and stepped into the hall.

It was empty. The shadows were too thin to hide anyone.

She listened for the creaks of Amira getting herself ready for bed, but the house was still.

She smelled the acrid tang of wet ashes, a breath of it, and then gone.

He was here. She knew it.

She finished washing up and padded back to the bedroom she had shared with Amira when they were children. Her father had never changed it. The dusty familiarity was less comforting than Felice thought it would be. She slid under the covers of her narrow twin bed and tucked her arms behind her head, watching the play of moonshadow on the ceiling.

"I wish we could live here again," she said into the silence. "Put it back the way it was."

"You really think that's possible?" Amira asked from the darkness beside her.

Felice caught the scent of a snuffed-out cigarette carried on a draft.

"I don't know. I think so," she answered, distracted. "Do you smell him? Right now?"

"I never smell anything, Felice."

Amira shifted position with a dry swish of sheets. Even in the dark, Felice could feel her sister's eyes on her. She knew Amira's pinched expression from the tone of her voice.

"I know you need to believe he's still here, that you can still find him all around, but it isn't real. And the more you tell yourself it is, the more you try to make me believe it is, the worse it is for you."

Felice kept her eyes focused on the ceiling.

"I like being back here. With you. Even like this," Felice said.

"I just want to go home," Amira answered. She sounded so far away.

"This used to be home," Felice said, pleading, turning to face her sister's dark shape. "Remember when he made us the rope swings?"

"Stop it," Amira said. "He's gone. Everything's gone. Everything changed years ago. Stop trying to keep some imaginary past alive."

Felice remained quiet, waiting until her sister eventually sighed and rolled over to sleep.

The rustle of her sheets released the faint sting of cigarette smoke.

Amira had never smoked.

Felice breathed in deeply, welcoming the smell.

"I'm here, Dad," she whispered into the night.

***

Felice rose before dawn. Despite the strange hour, Amira's bed was unused.

Felice crept quietly down to the kitchen, in case Amira had slept in a different room. She put up a kettle of water and opened the jar of instant coffee she had brought with her. She drowsed on her feet while she waited, looking out the window at the dark expanse of the yard. The kettle whined, and she lifted it to pour. As she turned, she thought she saw movement through the glass, and glanced up again at the window.

At her shoulder, her father's face faded into view, reflected against the failing night.

She jerked and the boiling water splashed out of the cup, spraying her hand. She shrieked and dropped the kettle. It clattered off the counter and onto the floor, a pool of hot water spreading from it.

"What have you done?" Amira shouted just behind her, stepping back from the steaming puddle.

"I saw him!" Felice cried, gripping her scalded hand.

Amira kept her distance from the mess.

"You did not see him. He's not here to see. It's not even five o'clock yet and you're still half-asleep."

"Amira, I saw his face in the glass, just before you came in."

Amira shook her head. "Stop trying to convince me. Let me see your hand."

Felice held her hand out to her sister, flinching against expected pain. Amira's fingers were ice cold where they stroked the rising blisters. The chill felt good against her burns.

"Thanks," Felice said. "That helps."

Amira let Felice's hand go and stepped back into the darkened hallway.

Felice took off her robe and used it to wipe up the spill. As she knelt on the worn linoleum, she sighed.

"He told me once that one of us was unplanned," Felice said. "Did you know that?"

"Unplanned?" Amira asked. "Or unwanted? Mama was never very warm toward either of us."

Felice looked at the wet fabric in her hands. It was already cold.

"No, she wasn't."

Felice tossed the robe into the corner near the sink and climbed to her feet.

"Dad was," she said to Amira, and paused. She swallowed before she went on. "You don't believe that I know things, that I can tell things," she said. "But I can."

"You don't know anything," Amira said, moving away. "You just need to feel special. But it's magical thinking. You should have grown out of it. None of us are special. None of us. Not really. No matter what we're told."

***

Later, Felice went back into her father's office. It felt less empty without Amira there, reminding her. She lay her cheek against the damp wallpaper again, closing her eyes, remembering how the room had looked when he was alive. When the world was a safe place. When she didn't know so many details.

When she hadn't been alone.

She stood at the desk and ran her hands over the damaged surface, hoping to find something she'd missed before. From behind her came a rustle of papers and a burst of sharp cold. She spun around, wanting.

As she watched, the ashes in the fireplace curled and crackled as they unburned, smoothing out into the dull squares of faded photographs that had fed the long-ago flames. Felice startled, delighted. She was right. She had known. She reached in gingerly, expecting heat. Instead, her hands sank into a pool of bitter cold. Her eyes teared as she leaned into it. Shivering, she scraped the reformed photos into a rough pile and pulled them out onto the hearth to look at.

The first few were baby pictures of a chubby, smiling infant in her crib, on a blanket on the lawn, in her mother's arms. Her mother. Their mother.

Felice looked at the picture in shock. Her mother smiled weakly at the camera, squinting against the summer sun, propping up her daughter at an awkward angle against her chest. Was the baby her, or Amira?

Why would her father have burned them?

Felice flipped through the rest, any joy draining from her. There was the one of her and Amira in matching crochet-lace dresses, taken when Felice was four and Amira two. There was the family picture taken one bright spring day on the wide back lawn, the year before her grandfather died. There was her high school graduation portrait. There was the photo of Amira with their father, the one she wanted to forget. It was taken that day.

Her mother left after that day, that unforgiven day, and left all the silences after.

The questions remained.

Felice stood up and kicked at the photos, scattering them across the rug and back into the fireplace.

The room grew bitterly cold around her as the freezing air billowed from the fireplace. Frost spread in a froth across the stone hearth and up the fireplace bricks. Felice heard the tiny pings of the mortar cracking under the sudden chill. Breath froze in her throat as she cried out. She slipped on the icy floor as she tried to turn away and fell heavily against the desk. Crushed against the sharp edge, her arm went numb.

She shoved herself up and ran for the door. The room seemed to stretch out before her like a bolt of cloth unspooling. She was out of breath when her hand closed on the door frame. She clung to it.

"What are you doing?" Amira called from upstairs.

Felice sagged against the frame, letting it hold her up.

"Felice?" Amira called again.

She tried to answer, but her mouth was suddenly too dry.

Amira's footsteps sounded quick and light on the stairs, growing louder and more solid as she came down the hall. Felice lifted her head, her face as stiff as a mask.

At first she could not see Amira. Her eyes would not focus. She shivered from the cold at her back. Then Amira was there.

"Why are you in here again?" Amira asked, reaching for her.

"You're lying if you say you can't sense it," Felice replied angrily, pulling away from her sister's hands.

"You don't know what you're saying," Amira said. "You don't know anything at all."

**

Felice waited until she thought Amira had to be asleep. She couldn't hear her breathing, even when she held her own breath.

She rose silently and tiptoed out of their bedroom, making her way by moonlight down the hall to her father's room. She eased the door closed behind her.

The moon stained the room with a wash of blue light. Felice walked forward into the abandoned space. There were no sorted piles. The room had been emptied. Felice rubbed her eyes, knowing she was awake. The wardrobe doors hung open, uneven on their hinges. She peered between them at a handful of wire clothes hangers left behind on the cabinet's bar.

A faint waft of old smoke enveloped her as she pulled them out and threw them on the floor.

**

"What happened to Dad's things?" Felice demanded, pulling the sheets off Amira's bed. The coming dawn made the light blurred and grey. She wasn't sure where the hours had gone.

"What do you mean?" Amira asked, rising.

"His room. Where are his things?"

"They're gone. They've been gone. Everything's gone."

"When did you get rid of them? I wasn't done!"

Amira shook her head.

"When did *I* get rid of them? You cling to this, this magic," she said, and walked out of their room.

Felice followed her.

The sun had only begun to creep over the horizon. The halls were full of shadows, and Amira a moving shadow among them. Felice struggled to keep up with her pace.

Amira led her down the hall, where her father's bedroom stood bare, the wardrobe gaping open, the bed stripped down to its frame. Felice groaned, unbelieving, as her sister's shadow passed her, turning back to the room they had shared. She followed again, searching for bearings. Now the matching twin beds were gone, and the dressers. Felice's travel bag sat open and forlorn on the worn carpet. She gasped and turned away.

Felice lost sight of Amira, even as the rooms grew slowly brighter. She steadied herself with the banister as she descended the stairs. She didn't need Amira. She had to see his office again. She had so many good memories of him there. If she could be there again she might be able to recall them, to know they were true.

When she entered, it was only an empty room. The cold snapped around her like teeth.

She sat down on the dirty hearth. There were no photographs in the fireplace. There were only ashes. There would only be ashes. She hung her head and sobbed.

Amira resolved from the waning shadows and stood over her sister in her grief. Felice rocked back and forth where she sat on the stones, her hair stuck to her face by tears and mucus.

"He's gone," she gasped out between sobs. "He's gone."

Amira opened a desk drawer and pulled out a dented pack of cigarettes. She lit one and held it out to Felice. After a moment of blank silence, Felice reached out and took it.

Amira's fingers were bitterly cold against her own.

Felice looked up. Amira smiled, her skin glittering, frost crackling over her lips.

"Yes," she said. "He's been gone for a long time. Longer than you'd think."

She lit another cigarette, exhaling a long plume of ice that shattered as it fell.

"And I'm still here."

THE GOLDEN HOUR

THOMAS WOKE ALONE and opened his sticky eyes to the dusty golden light that filled the bedroom. He expected to see Benjamin in the other bed, beside him, as if they were still children together. The bed was filled with familiar shadows, but Benjamin wasn't there. Instead, among their discarded toys he found another boy's body again.

His memory stuttered, caught on faces and places and angles of light, aromas and flavors that had long since faded to dust. He sighed and closed his bleary eyes against the visions.

He lifted the corpse with him when he rose, cradling it like a doll. He closed his eyes, and opened them again to see what he held, hoping all the years behind him had dissolved and made him new, hoping he would hold his brother. Sadness, swelling, filled him. His long hands released the boy's drained body, let it slump to the floor like empty clothes. He still saw the reflection of his brother's face in the boy's clouding eyes, his memory stronger than his sight.

***

He could hear their mother calling them to come in for dinner. He darted up the long back lawn, knowing that Benjamin was just behind him. He ran faster, to beat his brother to the porch.

But when he leapt to the top step and turned, grinning with triumph, Benjamin was just emerging from the trees that shadowed the stream running along the back of the property. The lingering golden dusk made a shadowy abstract of his face as he climbed the gentle slope to the house.

Thomas stood back as Benjamin came up the steps, unnerved by the brightness of his brother's eyes and the strange cheer in his voice.

"You beat me today," Benjamin said. "But it doesn't matter. I'll show you what I found in the stream tomorrow." And he went inside, where the lamplight disguised his new glow.

Thomas heard the clatter of dinner being put on the table. But he wasn't hungry for it.

**

As soon as their chores were done, Thomas followed his brother down to the stream. Benjamin still seemed lit from within, full of a marvelous secret.

What waited for them in the stream was as bright as a star, its pale, yellow light diffused beneath the rippling water. Thomas ran forward, reaching for it, but Benjamin pulled him back.

"No," Benjamin said, his eyes glistening, wet and shining with reflected radiance. "Be patient."

Thomas struggled to do as Benjamin said, fidgeting and scuffing his feet in the mud of the bank. But then the light bubbled up through the running stream, flowing up into the air above it on currents he could not feel even though he licked his palm and held it out to catch them.

Benjamin laughed at him and held his own hand out.

The brightness, translucent in the air, coiled up and around Benjamin's arm like a trained serpent. He laughed and lifted his shining arm toward his brother.

"What is it?" Thomas breathed.

Benjamin shook his head. "I don't know. It was just there, after you were gone."

He waved his arm through the air, the light clinging and trailing from it like lace.

"See?" Benjamin said. "It likes me!"

The light made a faint buzzing in the air, the noise of summer insects.

"Share it!" Thomas cried, hating the childish whine in his voice.

Thomas reached for it again, and Benjamin pulled his arm away.

"Let's see if it will come to you," he said, grinning. Thomas fought down raw resentment, waiting for his chance.

Benjamin stepped down into the stream and held his arm out. The light danced along it like fire on the edge of a blade, then wound its way back down his arm and around his body before gliding up into his smiling mouth. The light bubbled like laughter. Benjamin's teeth shone like gold.

Thomas could not contain himself any longer.

"It's not fair!" he shouted at Benjamin, and leaped at him. Benjamin lost his footing among the wet stones, and the two boys fell hard into the water. Benjamin squirmed, but Thomas was on top and fought to stay there. He got his hands around Benjamin's neck and squeezed as hard as he could, holding Benjamin under the water, watching the ripples distort his brother's screaming face as he struggled to breathe.

When Benjamin stopped fighting, Thomas took his hands from his throat and climbed, sodden, to his feet.

He looked down at the light streaming from his beneath his brother's closed lids, from his nostrils, his barely parted lips. He wanted it. The light was more beautiful than Benjamin could ever be.

Around him in the rushing water, the yellow light flashed and eddied and flowed away. He stumbled free of Benjamin's body to follow it down the streambed, but the water was quicker than he could be. Where the stream slowed and pooled and grew deeper, the light dissipated, dilute and invisible.

He waded back to where Benjamin lay, cold beneath the water.

Blood still seeped from Benjamin's skin where Thomas's digging hands had torn it, spinning threads along the currents. The blood glowed with remnants of the light, and without thought Thomas bent swiftly to scoop the shining, stained water up in his cupped hands, pouring handful after handful into his thirsty mouth. The blood was sour on his tongue, but he didn't stop. He felt the light spark inside him. He was aglow with it, alive, more alive than he had been.

When the water flowed clean again, he stopped and wiped his mouth with his sleeve.

Benjamin's eyes had opened in the moving stream, and his eyes stared up blindly at the trees above them. The daylight grew softer as the evening drew down, and Benjamin's pale face looked like a pearl.

Thomas bent over his brother and prodded him with his toe. Benjamin lolled along the streambed, cradled in the stones. Water swirled his auburn hair in strange patterns around his empty face.

Thomas began to weep then, his anger fled, suddenly aware of what he had done and what trouble he had made.

He stood in the water for a long time, his feet numb in the chilly stream, his eyes sore from crying. As it grew darker, he could not help himself from looking for any glint of the light. There was none. Even Benjamin's face had become as dull as the stones he lay on.

When he heard his mother calling for them, he slogged out of the stream and made his way slowly back to the house. The green-yellow pulses of fireflies lit his way up the long back lawn through the failing day. In their flickering, he imagined Benjamin walked beside him, as he always had.

He did not know what he would tell her when he got home.

***

He stayed in the house alone while the neighbors brought Benjamin's body up from the stream.

He could hear his mother's keening clearly in the still summer air, rising and falling like a siren as she drew in breath. That night he listened to her sob steadily in her bed as he watched the faint tracery of light move under his skin. The glow was already fading.

The endless night wore on. He could not sleep. He had never been apart from Benjamin in their thirteen years. He rose quietly and walked through the rooms of their small house like a lost lamb, hating Benjamin for his light and missing him, missing him.

***

Thomas tried to escape the grim show of his brother's funeral, but his mother laid Benjamin out in the front parlor and made him sit quietly in the wing chair beside the closed coffin. Thomas wondered if it were filled with light seeping from his brother's body. He kept his eyes down, not really wanting to know the answer.

His mother and the preacher spoke in hushed voices in the doorway as the hours dragged on. He heard her whispering, *No, no,* to the preacher's questions, and drawing him into prayer to stop him asking any more. No one else came to call, not even the neighbors who had carried him up from the stream, until the mortician arrived in the afternoon to take Benjamin to his grave.

The carriage ride was solemn, with only the sound of the horses to break the hot summer stillness.

At the graveyard, the preacher said the proper words while his mother cried into her handkerchief, hugging Thomas against her hip, as if he would die, too, if she didn't. Then Benjamin was lowered into the hole dug next to their father's grave, and the ceremony was over.

His mother clutched the handful of dirt she was to have thrown onto Benjamin's coffin, refusing to help bury her boy. She held onto it until they were back home again and the preacher gently pried her hand open and brushed the dirt onto the front step.

"Dust to dust, Elly," he said, patting her shoulder and casting a sharp glance at Thomas before climbing into his buggy and heading back to town.

When they were alone, she hugged Thomas tightly again and then went to her room and shut the door. She did not come out for supper. He lit the lamps and sat on the porch, watching the stars flare and fade in the deep, deep sky.

Before dawn came, he made his way on foot back to the burial plot and brought Benjamin home.

***

Although his mother forbade it, he would not stay away from the stream. She huddled in her bed and made no move to stop him, only begged him in a thin, frightened whine not to go, not to leave her too. Day after day he made his way down to the water, her plaintive protests growing faint behind him until he could not hear her at all.

Each day he pulled a stone from the stream and added it to the cairn he built over Benjamin's body to keep it from the animals. The pile was almost as high as his waist now, and the summer was growing short.

He knew if the light had come once, it would come again. He more than knew. He was sure of it.

And one day he was right.

As he set another stone over his brother that heavy morning, he caught a flash in the water, too golden for the sun so early in the day.

He crouched on the bank, cautious of scaring it away. Slowly, so slowly, he leaned toward it, dipping his fingers into the stream and holding them there, waiting for the light to find them. Benjamin was not able to lure it from him now.

The light flickered in the water, flashes and streaks like silver minnows darting to and then away from his hands. He leaned out farther, grasping at the insubstantial. He wanted it with his whole heart, wanted it so much he forgot how much he hated Benjamin for being its chosen vessel.

He slipped from the muddy bank and fell, still reaching for the light. His head struck a stone that sat higher than the others, and the ringing pain drove him out of himself. His mouth and nose filled with cool water, and when he gasped at the weight of it the water choked him, dimming his sight, closing his throat. He lay still in the chilly stream for hours, aware of the sun moving above him, of the singing birds darting through the trees, of the small fish that explored his open eyes, his open mouth.

The light was in him.

He lay there, cold, and reveled in it.

As the sun began to set, he heard his mother calling, more loudly than she had before. Closer than she had been. She was looking for him.

"Thomas!" she called, her voice high and shrill. "Where are you?"

He could hear the fear in her voice, that she should lose her last son too.

Around him, the stream grew dark, the golden light washing away. He stood without grace, as if he inhabited his body for the first time, and climbed carefully up the slick bank toward where she waited for him.

It was far harder than he expected.

The light in him died as the day died, and he felt himself dying with it. The dimming became a dull ache in his muscles, his bones. His limbs felt distant, disconnected and not his own. He lay down beside Benjamin's cairn, too tired to stand, until his mother's approaching pleas forced him to his feet again. He moved.

She cried out when she saw him shambling across the lawn in the violet dusk, wet and disjointed. She ran to him, her dressing gown flapping around her, and gathered him to her, drying his face with her skirts. He felt her shudder when she found the long, bloodless gash at his hairline. He saw the fear in her eyes, the instinctive animal doubt that he was only injured.

"Let's get you home," she said, her voice breaking. She kept her eyes away from his face, from his injury. She held him close to her side and steadied him as they walked back up to the house.

***

The stream did not compel him any longer. He wanted what was gone, what he did not know how to get. In his indeterminacy, he stayed near his mother. She needed him near, a reassurance that she was not alone. Sometimes, she called him Benjamin. Sometimes, he would let himself be Benjamin, for her. He knelt at her feet as she read to him, to Benjamin, from Genesis, Leviticus, Psalms, and Acts. He listened to her phlegmy voice but there was no atonement for him to make, no prayer to release him. She read the words aloud anyway, her voice a proof of her belief and a solace against his quiet shape.

But he had already learned a different lesson. He knew what had happened to him, there in the stream. The light in the blood was a lie, a promise that could not ever be fulfilled, a fleeting respite from the truth of the grave. He grew used to the incessant hunger for it, unsated.

Seasons passed. His mother grew frail and frightened of him. He did not age, but he changed all the same. How long did his mother believe he was still with her, still alive, he wondered. And how much longer did she tell herself he still was, even after she knew it was false?

She tried to make him explain it to her, more than once, what was different, what he had become. He could not. He would not try. When, after years of his silences, she coughed, and cried, and fell lifeless from her chair, he felt a strange relief that she would not demand answers of him ever again.

He put her in the remains of her flower garden, which she had loved. And he brought Benjamin up from the stream bank, to share the house with him again.

***

They were forgotten, he thought, when he thought of anything else. He could not remember any neighbors, not after so long. The road to the house was overgrown, its line broken by strong young trees. The fields, too, filled with weeds and saplings swaying in the sun. All that remained was the house, weathered white and crack-windowed. And him. He remained. He grew used to the loneliness.

He would sit in the sunlight, on the long grass, basking like a lizard in its heat. The skin pulled tight across his face, drying to brown leather. He did not look in the filmy mirror anymore. He knew what he looked like.

His was still shaped like the boy he had been that summer day, but his skin sagged in brittle brown folds and his limbs were like sticks. He had clung to his semblance of life for so long that his form had crumpled and distorted under the weight of the years. His eyes had become damp, shrunken stones in his face, his teeth fangs that cut through his papery cheeks. He thought if he lay in the overgrown garden he would be overlooked as a pile of broken branches.

While the days passed, he lay there, and watched, and waited to see who might find the forgotten old house. There had always been a few, travelers or adventuring souls. Until they came, he would close his eyes and talk with Benjamin, believing.

***

When the first child pried open the warped kitchen door and explored the house with adolescent bravado, Thomas waited in his bed, hidden like a spider, anxious and uncertain of what would come. When the boy walked cautiously into the shaded bedroom, Thomas saw the golden light, the elusive light, shining through the boy's skin.

At that instant, the boy looked like Benjamin. Thomas's vision blurred and scattered, wanting his brother again.

He leapt up from his bed with an inconsolable urgency and snatched at the boy's hair, his shirt, his face, clawing at him and knocking him to the floor. He dug in with nails and teeth, splitting open the shining skin, gulping down the gouting blood, slaking his thirst on the light.

He wanted, he wanted. He could not swallow fast enough. His mouth, his throat, his belly full, full to bursting, he could feel the light within him surging hot and already fading.

When the violent passion burned itself out, he looked down at the scraps of flesh he still clutched, at the torn face, at the wasted blood. The light was going from it now, but he could feel it moving through his own veins, dimmed but still potent.

The boy did not look like Benjamin at all.

He gathered up the remains and buried them at the bottom of the yard.

If one curious child had come, he thought, there would be others.

He could wait, dormant as a dried seed waiting for rain. He had been hungry before.

Between the brief sparks that found him, he lay still, without strength, filled with nothing but want of the light. He was always wanting, even as he slept. The light never lasted, not in him. Never in him.

***

He buried the new body with all the others, at the edge of the grass just before the trees began. The sun made the skin on his neck and back crackle as he bent to his task. He made the grave shallow. He did not know how long the light within him would last, how long he would be strong enough to walk to the stream, to bask in the afternoon light, to bury the body. He did not want to waste what was inside him.

He could just make out the boy's features through the sparse screen of dirt. The boy had been beautiful, before he was dead. As beautiful as Benjamin had been. But his eyes saw what his memory would not. The boy was not Benjamin. None of the boys had been Benjamin. He closed his faithless eyes and let his thoughts flutter loose again. If he did not look, then his brother was there with him, at least for a moment, an hour, perhaps a day. He was no longer angry that he had kept him from the light that day. Benjamin had surely known better.

He lay down beside the graves. The warm, honeyed summer sun felt good on his thin brown skin. He only remembered summer now, not the pale mist of spring or the sinking chill of autumn becoming winter. Summer was when Benjamin was still alive.

He stayed there all afternoon, remembering, reliving, until the blue shadows stretched across the lawn and, cold, he rose to face the waning light. Beside him, where his brother should have been, were only dusty bones.

ꟼUBLICATION HISTORY

Green Girl *first appeared on PodCastle, October 2016*
Queen In Red *first appeared in Rose Red Review, Fall 2013*
Alba *first appeared in AnotherRealm, April 2016*
For the Night Is Long, and I Am Lost Without You *first appeared in Vastarien Volume 5 Issue 1, June 2022*
And Lucy Fell *first appeared in Nightmare Magazine #101, February 2021*
Compline *first appeared in Harbinger, November 2019*
To Selareme *first appeared in Lost Atlantis Short Stories, September 2023*
Seven Stars *first appeared in Uncharted Magazine, September 2021*
Cut in Marble/Pasiphaë *first appeared in Eternal Haunted Summer, Summer 2015*
As Below, So Above *first appeared in Lamplight Volume 9 Issue 1, October 2020*
Seals *first appeared in Windward, October 2016*
The Wind, the Sand *first appeared on Tales to Terrify Episode 453, October 2020*
The Fire This Time *first appeared in Turn To Ash Volume 0, September 2016*
Predation *first appeared in Triangulation: Appetites, July 2017*
Waiting for the Worms *first appeared in Generation X-Ed, January 2022*
To Die, to Sleep, No More *first appeared in Weirdbook Annual: Zombies!, October 2021*
Out with the Old *first appeared in Daily Science Fiction, October 2021*
World Enough, and Time *first appeared in Future Visions, June 2018*
Something After *first appeared in A Quaint and Curious Volume of Gothic Tales, January 2022*
The Golden Hour *first appeared in Nightmare Magazine #114, March 2022*

ABOUT THE AUTHOR

ERICA RUPPERT (HWA, SFWA) lives in northern New Jersey with her husband and too many cats. She is the author of two novellas, *Sisters in Arms* and *To the Shore, to the Sea*, and has published over sixty short stories. Her debut collection, *Imago and Other Transformations*, was released by Trepidatio Publishing in 2023. When she is not writing, she runs, bakes, and gardens with more enthusiasm than skill.